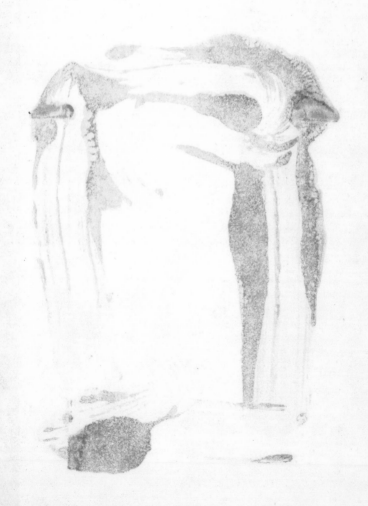

The King's Road

THE
KING'S
ROAD

Cecelia Holland

Illustrated by Richard Cuffari

Atheneum   New York
1970

75/6-m - 154

The King's Road

FEDERIGO settled himself comfortably on the branch and peeled another orange. The juice of the first had made his chin and fingers sticky, and the heavy, tart odor filled his nostrils. Among the masses of dark green leaves all around him, he could see the ripe fruit hanging like golden balls—like the tree in the legend, that grew at the end of the world. He tore off half the peel and sank his teeth into the sun-warmed pulp, and more juice flowed over his chin and splashed on his shirt.

Through the branches, he had a good view of the road that ran along the plain just beyond the wall of the orchard; he could see a little band of horsemen riding up from the city of Palermo toward the royal palace of Al-Aziz. Among the bay and chestnut horses, a white mule trotted. That would be a Papal Legate—an ambassador of the Pope to Sicily. Monks always rode white mules. Federigo gulped orange juice and watched them ride carefully along the rocky road, followed by a small group of boys from the

3

city. The boys were running in and out of the troop of horses, shouting. Federigo could tell that the men were getting angry.

"Whoever's up in that tree, come down or I'll give you a beating."

Startled, Federigo nearly fell off the branch. He looked around until he saw the man who had yelled—the big, gray-bearded farmer who owned the orchard, and who was striding forward with a pole raised threateningly in his hand. The boy wiped his chin hastily on his sleeve.

"Don't worry, Master, it's only me—Federigo." He swung down from the branch, hung a moment at arm's length, and dropped to the ground almost on top of the farmer.

"Oh, well," the man said, and smiled. "They're good oranges, aren't they?" He reached out and tousled Federigo's hair. "Why don't you come in the front gate next time?"

Federigo grinned. "Because it's more fun to climb the wall, Master. They're beautiful oranges." He turned and started toward the wall at a trot.

"I'll send you some if you want," the farmer called.

"Don't do that." Federigo jumped and caught the top of the stone wall, hitched himself up, and swung around to sit on the edge. "Diepold would only eat them all."

He waved, and the farmer laughed and went back through the trees toward his little white house, which Federigo could just make out beyond the orderly rows of the orange trees.

The procession of the Papal Legate was drawing nearer, still accompanied by the swarm of boys. Beneath the plodding hoofs of the horses, the dust rose in a fine, golden cloud, lit by the late sun. One of the Legate's knights was bellowing and waving at the boys, trying to shoo them off; his broad red face glowed with bad temper. Federigo crossed his legs and watched, grinning. He knew the boys, he played with them all the time; and the threats and curses of a pack of knights wouldn't drive them back one inch. His hands were covered with sticky orange juice and bits of peel and pulp, which he tried to wipe off on his shirt.

Astride his mule, the Papal Legate looked uncomfortable and angry. Federigo tucked his legs under him and watched. The Pope was the overlord of the King of Sicily, and Papal Legates were always coming down to Palermo, but this one was a stranger to him. The man on the white mule drew abreast of him and reined up, scowling. His pale eyes glared at Federigo.

"Is Sicily peopled with nothing but beggar boys?"

Federigo grinned. He knew how he looked—covered with dust and orange scraps, his red hair standing on end— and he could tell that the Papal Legate didn't know who he was.

He called, "Excellency, are they bothering you?" and gestured toward the howling mob of boys dashing in and out of the group of knights. "If they are, I'll send them away."

The Legate's fat red face turned redder still. His fine clothes, studded with jewels, were covered with a film of dust, and blisters showed on his hands; obviously he wasn't used to handling the reins even of a mule.

He said, "Thank you, no. I'd advise you to get down from there before someone comes along to throw you off."

"Oh, nobody would do that." Federigo cocked his head to one side. "Why are you going to Al-Aziz?"

The Legate sputtered angrily. "Now, see here, I'm not about to talk state business with beggars in the street. Get along with you."

"You can talk about it to me." Federigo leaped casually down from the wall. He walked over to the mule, which tried to bite him, and slapped its muzzle. The Legate gasped, and a few of the knights muttered in surprise. "I'll go up there with you," Federigo said cheerfully, "if you'll give me a horse to ride."

The other boys had gathered behind Federigo and were quiet. He glanced around to grin at them. Durante was there, and Yusuf. He swung back when the Legate said angrily, "Why should I give you a horse to ride?"

"Because," Federigo said, "my name is Federigo, and I'm the King of Sicily. I'll take that bay horse, there."

The knights all around the Legate stared at him, and the Legate turned pale. His mouth worked nervously. Covered with dirt, shaggy-headed and barefoot, the boys crowded around Federigo.

Yusuf called, "Little Red, are they from Rome?"

"I think so," Federigo said. "They certainly look like it."

The Legate was telling the knight on the bay horse to dismount and ride double with someone else.

Durante drew closer to Federigo and whispered, "Make them give us something. The Pope is rich."

"I can't," Federigo said softly. "They'd tell Diepold, and Diepold would have me whipped." He made a face. The knight had gotten off the bay horse, and Federigo started toward it, through the packed horses of the other knights.

Over his shoulder, he called, "I'll see you sometime tomorrow, Durante." Running up to the bay horse, he took the reins from the knight and judged the distance from the ground to the stirrup—it was a huge horse.

"Let me help you mount, Your Grace," the knight said.

"Don't bother." Federigo leaped up, grabbed the pommel of the saddle, and stabbed his foot into the stirrup. With a lurch he swung his other leg over the high cantle of the saddle and sat upright, his feet dangling far above the stirrups. "Thank you." He grinned down at the knight. Getting the reins firmly in his hands, he kicked the horse and let out a whoop that made the Legate's mule rear up, snorting. The bay horse took off like an arrow, straight up the road. The knights yelled, and the boys screamed in delight. Looking back, Federigo saw that the Legate had fallen off his mule, and he laughed and steered the horse toward the gate of the palace, standing open in the bright midafternoon sun.

"And you got yourself all dirty again," said Franciscus, who was Federigo's tutor. "Can't you ever remember that you are the King?"

Federigo let the old man take off his shirt. "I think about it all the time. Why is the Legate here from Rome?"

Franciscus bundled up the shirt in a ball and threw it onto a pile of laundry. "Ask my lord Diepold, he'll tell you." He rummaged through the closet for a clean shirt. Federigo sat down on the bed. He and Franciscus shared three rooms in the oldest, coldest part of the palace, far from everything else.

"He won't. He says I'm too young to worry about things

like that and tells me to go play. I'm twelve, that's old enough to know what happens in my Kingdom." A little thread of doubt ran through his mind. "Isn't it?"

"Well," Franciscus said, turning. He held up a clean shirt and inspected it in the fading light from the window. "You're the oldest twelve-year-old I've ever seen. Do you suppose you can keep from ripping this one again? It's almost past mending."

"I thought Elissa was going to make me more shirts." Federigo rose and stood with his hands over his head so that Franciscus could put the shirt on.

"She was, but Diepold wouldn't give her the money for the cloth."

"I'll see if I can get some."

Franciscus tugged the shirt straight and laced it up the front. "I've told you you mustn't do that. The merchants who would give you something are all poor. The rich never give anything away, that's how they get rich. And you mustn't be a burden to the poor."

Federigo trotted to the window and leaned out to watch the sun go down. In the park below him, a few tame deer were grazing in the sweet grass of the meadow.

"I could steal it."

He heard Franciscus move just in time to brace himself; the old man grabbed him by the shoulder and shook him vigorously.

"Don't you ever steal anything. Kings don't steal, either."

"Kings steal all the time. They try to take each other's Kingdoms, don't they?" He let Franciscus shake him, because it made the old man feel that he was teaching him something. Franciscus was a very forceful tutor.

"That's not stealing," Franciscus said. "That's war." His hand slipped from Federigo's shoulder, and he sighed. "How can I teach you anything when everything you see teaches you precisely the opposite?"

"You tell me what's right, and they show me what's wrong."

"I'm glad you know that."

Federigo said nothing. Before his eyes, the sunset spread rose and lilac over the sky, and the white stone towers of the city beyond the palace wall turned colors: minarets and church towers and the peaks of synagogues catching the last light of the sun. He had been King of Sicily since he'd been three, just before his mother's death. His father had died a year after he was born. In the nine years since his coronation, men like Diepold had fought each other to control the kingdom and make themselves rich; they'd kidnapped Federigo, because whoever held the King held the right to rule. Henry VII, Federigo's father, had been the Emperor of the Germans; and if Henry had lived long enough, Federigo would have followed him to the Imperial throne, but now he was Diepold's pawn. He watched the sun glide down behind the sea, and the sky darkened to a deep, beautiful purple-blue, picked out with the first stars. He had always known that orphans had no power to control their lives.

"I'll ask Diepold myself for money for new shirts," he said. He knew it would get them nothing—Diepold didn't much care what condition Federigo was in, so long as Diepold had him around to sign papers and appear at court receptions, like the one tonight.

"You might ask him for kitchen money, too," Franciscus said crisply. "You're perfectly capable of feeding yourself, I know, but for an old man it's not so easy to sneak into orchards and beg on street corners."

Federigo blushed and lowered his head. He'd forgotten that Franciscus had to eat as well. Usually he brought something back for the old man, but today the excitement of the procession had chased the thought from his head. "I teased the Papal Legate today and that made me forget. I'm sorry."

Gently, Franciscus said, "Don't worry. Elissa sometimes brings me dishes from Diepold's own table. I probably eat better than you do." He went over to light a stub of candle on the wall.

"Well, then," Federigo said, grinning, "I'll stop bringing you anything at all." He swung around.

Franciscus had gotten out the fancy coat, trimmed with shredded gold and embroidered with the arms of Sicily and Hohenstaufen.

"I'm afraid this ceremony is going to go on all night. Have you studied your Latin?"

"Amo, amas, amat. Yes." Federigo helped him put the coat over his head and do up the jeweled clasps. "And I read all the German and nearly all the history."

"What about the mathematics?" Franciscus knelt stiffly to brush off the coat.

"I did that, too." Mathematics was his easiest subject; he never did his lessons beforehand, but figured out the problems in his head while Franciscus was checking up the answers on the last page of the text. There was a knock on the door.

"Who is it?" Franciscus called, hastily standing up.

The door opened, and Lothair, one of Diepold's favorites, came into the room, swaying so that his gorgeous red robes sparkled in the candlelight.

"Is the King ready?"

Federigo went over to the table in the corner, where the little cherrywood chest with his ornaments stood. His coat was long enough that he didn't have to wear shoes.

"Just a moment."

Lothair always made him angry and watchful—Lothair hit him sometimes, when Diepold ordered him punished. Inside the chest lay all the jewels his mother had given him, the signet rings and chains and medals, and loose gems, blue sapphires, emeralds, rubies like drops of blood. The signet ring of the Kingdom of Sicily wasn't there, Diepold had it and couldn't rule without it. He took the big medal on its silver chain and hung it around his neck.

"Now I'm ready."

"Come along, then," Lothair said impatiently. "They're all waiting."

Franciscus was staring at Lothair with a frown on his face. Federigo walked carefully, so that his bare feet wouldn't show under the hem of the coat, and followed Lothair out the door.

"The Papal Legate is named Giovanni da Capa," Lothair said, walking fast and looking straight ahead. "In addition to the customary nobles and officers, Walter of Brienne is present in the court. He's the tall—"

"I know him," Federigo said. He trotted to keep up. Walter of Brienne had been exiled a long time before, he couldn't remember when, although he could visualize the man's long horse face in his mind. Diepold had ordered him exiled, had wanted him killed, but now Walter was back. Something was going on, something he surely ought to know about but did not. In the small chamber outside the hall, he stopped and looked up at the arms of his House, hanging on the wall over the hearth. Lothair went off to talk to someone else. The room was packed with chairs and tables, at which secretaries sat writing and studying sheafs of documents. Other men, in velvet and satin and silk, stood or sat or wandered through the room, followed by pages. No one paid any attention to Federigo. He leaned against the stone wall between two tapestries and watched them carefully. What they did, these men—whom they decided to trust and whom to obey, whom to hate and fight—determined what would happen to him. Diepold couldn't rule without them, the landholding barons and their servants; if he displeased them they would turn against him and make someone else Regent. I'm helpless, he thought, with a surge of anger. I can't do anything except what they wish of me. He watched the Duke of Foligno, short, thin, balding, stop at a secretary's desk and say something. When he turned away, his cold eyes grazed Federigo and didn't stop; he looked at Federigo as if he didn't exist. Federigo bit his lower lip.

Diepold came in, surrounded by pages and soldiers. His coat was stiff with jewels and bits of precious metal, and on his huge, meaty hands rings flashed constantly. Federigo straightened up. Now the reception for the Legate would start. Diepold was German, like Federigo's father, with whom he'd come to Sicily. His broad, heavy face always looked as if he were a little sick to his stomach. His skin was stretched so tightly over the bones of his face that it shone, and his mouth was permanently twisted into a sour grimace. Everybody else in the room turned and watched him. Some bowed—the minor nobles, who had to seek his favor. In the midst of it all, Diepold stopped and turned ponderously, looking around. When he saw Federigo leaning against the wall, he nodded, looked to a man beside him, and said, "You may tell the Legate the reception is about to begin. The King is here."

Federigo walked toward Diepold, circling around a clump of nobles and pages in the livery of Tommaso of Celano, the Count of Molise, who was so powerful he didn't even have to come to major court events.

Diepold looked grimly down at Federigo. The regent had been a knight once, of no rank and little influence, just a wandering knight; his thick bones and long, strong legs and hands looked out of place against his rich clothes and the jewels he wore, like a work horse in fancy harness.

"Well, little King," he said, "ready for the ordeal?" He clapped Federigo on the shoulder, almost affectionately. "Pay attention and do as I say, and everything will go well."

"Yes, sir."

Trumpets blared. Two pages rushed up to Federigo. One straightened his coat and the other carried a velvet cushion with Federigo's crown on it—a simple gold coronet, since the real crown was too heavy for any but a grown man to wear. Diepold reached out and took the crown. For a moment he held it, looking down at it. Federigo watched him expressionlessly. Diepold's face tightened and grew fierce. Federigo clenched his fist against his side. Diepold had all the power to rule, but not the crown, and without the crown he would eventually lose his power. Someday Federigo himself would be old enough to rule. But if Diepold could only take the crown as well . . .

"That's mine." Federigo thrust out his hands and took the gold circlet from Diepold.

"So it is." Diepold frowned at him. "Put it on so we can go in."

Brushing his long hair back, Federigo put the crown on his head. The trumpets blasted again, and in a little procession, with soldiers first and Federigo walking ahead of Diepold, they entered the great hall.

Beneath the rows of pennants and the smoky, stinking torches, standing in a neat row on the rush-covered floor before the throne, the Papal Legate and his party waited. They bowed. Federigo walked up the stair to his throne, swung around, and drew a deep breath. Across the room a tall, thin man smiled and bowed within a ring of his own servants—Walter of Brienne. Federigo saw Diepold and Walter look at each other warily, like dogs circling before they fought.

"Lords, ladies, gentlemen and people of Sicily, most excellent Giovanni da Capa of Rome, ambassador of the Most Holy Innocent III," the herald shouted, "you are in the presence of the King of Sicily, Frederick Roger von Hohenstaufen, duke of Apulia, duke of Calabria—" He ran off the rest of Federigo's titles, while everyone stood stiffly at attention and pretended to listen. Federigo's ankle itched, and he scratched it carefully with the other foot. The herald ended his speech and rapped his staff on the floor, and Federigo sat down.

Giovanni da Capa stood forward and delivered a small speech, praising the beauty and peace of Sicily and stating the Pope's interest in his vassal's kingdom. Federigo didn't bother to listen. They always said the same things, like a ritual, like going to church, and what they said had no relation to what they meant or wanted. Diepold made another speech, welcoming Giovanni and assuring him that Sicily loved the Pope and Holy Mother Church more than anything else. Which wasn't true either, because Diepold was always cheating on his reports of revenues due the Church and on occasion had actually stolen the money of priests and monasteries. Federigo settled himself in the cold throne and played with the lions and eagles carved into the arms.

"Your Grace." It was Walter of Brienne, smiling, leaning up against the side of the throne. "You've grown since I last saw you. It's good to see you looking so well, Sire."

"Thank you, Lord Walter."

"You remember me. I'm flattered."

The Papal Legate was approaching. Federigo tried quickly to figure out why Walter was talking to him, why Walter was putting on such a show of interest, and decided that the Papal Legate had something to do with it. The Legate stopped on the steps of the throne, his eyes on Federigo, but when he spoke it was to Walter.

"The Sicilians have a most charming and intelligent young King. I can see why you wish to return, Lord Walter."

Federigo twitched. It sounded as if Walter was not back for good, but just to visit. He looked around for Diepold and saw him watching the two men by the throne with keen eyes.

"His Holiness the Pope will be pleased to know how Your Grace fares under the tutelage of Lord Diepold," the Legate said.

Federigo's eyes returned to him; he said nothing. They were trying to make him say something against Diepold—perhaps that Diepold mistreated him. The Legate's smile sagged limply after a moment, but Walter's looked as bright as ever.

"If there is anything you might wish His Holiness to know," Walter said, "you may tell the Legate without any chance of your opinions reaching the wrong ears, Your Grace."

On Federigo's head, the crown pressed heavily. He thought, I could get back at Diepold for all the . . . But he knew that he would not. These men weren't trying to help him, but only to gain some advantage for themselves. He looked curiously from the Legate to Walter and back again, wondering how they could be so obvious and hope to get anywhere with it. Across the room, a woman laughed loudly.

"Surely," Walter said, "there must be something you have to tell your guardian? After all, Sire, the Pope is your foster parent."

Federigo stared at him a little longer and nodded. "Yes. Excellency, you may tell His Holiness that I am studying devoutly and I pray every day to be allowed to be the kind of king who will do credit to Holy Mother Church." He smiled at them—they looked so crestfallen. "When I am King in fact as well as name."

Walter's forehead creased into three deep wrinkles. "Is

Lord Diepold treating you properly?"

"As properly as I've ever been treated."

He nearly laughed. They'd expected him to cry to them, so that they would have some tale of misery and injustice to take to the Pope and use against Diepold. In a doorway behind Diepold's cluster of friends, Franciscus appeared and waved.

"Excuse me, I think it's my bedtime." He got up, holding onto the crown with one hand to keep it from slipping off. Diepold stirred and raised his head when Federigo walked down the steps from the throne, and seeing Federigo start for the door, he moved to intercept him. The boy stopped, watching Diepold come toward him, his hands on his hips.

"Franciscus is there; I have to go to bed," Federigo said, looking up at Diepold.

The big German stopped in front of him. The silver and gold woven into his coat flashed in the torchlight. Federigo could smell sour wine on his breath; he recoiled slightly.

"What did you tell them?" Diepold said softly. He sank down on his heels and put one hand on Federigo's arm. His eyes blazed. "What did they ask you?"

Furious, Federigo jerked his arm out of Diepold's fingers. "Don't touch me."

Diepold's eyes narrowed to slits. "What did they ask you?" With a quick jerk of his head, he looked around to see if anybody was watching. They all were, but no one was close enough to overhear.

"They asked if I had anything to complain about," Federigo said. Under the fancy collar of his coat, Diepold's neck was flecked with fleabites. Federigo was disgusted—he hated fleas and lice and took a bath every day to make sure he had none. He gritted his teeth.

"What did you say?" Diepold asked.

"Nothing. Let me go, Franciscus is waiting for me."

Diepold looked puzzled. He put one hand out to touch Federigo, who moved back out of reach. Diepold's hand fell to his knee.

"Why? You could have poured your heart out to them, they would have loved it."

Federigo's head ached from the weight of the crown. He put both hands up and took it off. The touch of the cold metal in his palms made him feel stronger, and he said, "You would do that, Diepold, but I wouldn't." His throat tightened up; he hated this, not being able to do anything for himself, being at their mercy. Now they were trying to make him play their silly game. He stared at Diepold a moment longer and ran around him and toward the door. A page came up to him just before he reached Franciscus.

"Your Grace—let me take the crown—"

Federigo stopped. His fingers tightened around the crown, and he thought of telling the page he couldn't have it. But they'd only take it away. And the crown itself meant nothing; Diepold could wear it all he wanted, but it would never make him King, not while Federigo lived. He handed the page the crown and turned to Franciscus.

"The Pope has sent you a letter," Franciscus said. His arm went around the boy's shoulders. "It's in Latin—we can translate it tomorrow for your lesson." His fingers smoothed Federigo's sleeve. "Come to bed now. You'll have bad dreams if you stay up late."

Federigo let the old man draw him out the door into the next room. "What are they doing? Is the Pope going to send Diepold away?"

"He's trying, apparently. It will probably work, too." Franciscus helped him unclasp the coat and took it off, folding it over his arm. "Heaven help us, Federigo. Did you go in there without shoes on?"

"They didn't notice."

Franciscus sighed. Together they walked through the empty, darkened rooms toward their part of the palace. Federigo's bare feet crunched on the rushes on the floor, and without the coat he could feel the cool draft from the walls. They walked through a little room where Federigo sometimes had to sign charters; the tapestries were rippling slightly in the breeze. Suddenly Federigo felt tired to his bones.

"Why don't they ever let me alone?" He was holding Franciscus by the arm, and he leaned on the old man, pushing his head against Franciscus' side.

"Ssssh. You're too old to whine. Here." Franciscus took a tart out of his sleeve and thrust it into Federigo's hand. "Eat this, it's good to go to bed on a full stomach."

The tart's thick sweet crust broke under Federigo's teeth, and he tasted cherry jam. While they climbed the dark, cold stairs he ate the tart, savoring each bite, and licked the juice from his fingers. Long after they'd reached the head of the stairs and the tart was gone, he could taste cherry jam in his mouth. With Franciscus' arm around him, he went to his room. So the Pope had sent him another letter. He always rattled on and on with advice and little stories from

the Bible as examples of good conduct. He yawned. Tomorrow was just the other side of sleeping; tomorrow he
would read the Pope's letter, and tomorrow he would go to
see David ben Isaac. He let Franciscus lead him in and help
him take his clothes off.

THE BRILLIANT SUN beat down on the little white houses on either side of the street; Federigo moved into the shade of an old olive tree. The street ran down a steep hill to the harbor, and at the far end of it he could see the glitter of the water. A ripple of pleasure coursed through him. The air smelled of the olive tree and the warm stone of the houses, and occasionally the wind brought him the noise of the bazaar in the next alley: a chatter of high-pitched voices, the sound of donkeys and goats and cattle moving around, and the rumble of wagon wheels. He wiggled his bare toes deeper into the dust. He didn't have to be back until sundown, and it was barely noon. He could play, talk to people, beg oranges and candy in the bazaars, watch the ships in the harbor, anything he wanted. He trotted out into the blazing sun again and ran down the hill, his arms widespread and his shirt flapping around his ribs.

The steep slope helped him on, faster than he could normally run, his strides gigantic. Halfway down to the bot-

24

tom, he saw an ox cart turn into the street at the next corner. He tried to stop himself and could not; he lost his balance, tripped, and fell onto the rough cobblestones. Rolling, he flung out his arms to stop himself. In the cart a man shouted a warning. Federigo rolled up against a wall, at a place where leaves and dirt had drifted up in a little heap to cushion the blow, and sat up, dazed.

The man on the cart shouted, "Watch out, boy, I nearly hit you." He waved his long whip. The cream-colored ox, dragging the cart on up the hill, swung its big head to stare at him, moist-eyed.

Federigo laughed. When the cart had gone by, he picked himself up and jogged across the street to a doorway. He'd torn his shirt, and his knees and hands hurt viciously. Standing under the swinging wooden sign above the door, he inspected the scrapes on his palms. Small drops of blood oozed slowly through the torn skin. He wiped his hands on his trousers and went into the shop.

Inside, it was unexpectedly cool, and everything smelled of old leather and ink and wood. For a moment, he could see nothing in the darkness, and he blinked to get his eyes used to it. In the dim, quiet room, he could hear the scratching of a pen over parchment and the shuffling of feet. Gradually, he began to pick out details—Feisal, David ben Isaac's helper, sitting on his high stool in front of a desk, and the piles of books and boxes and the general litter of pens and parchment. Ink in big jars filled the shelves against one wall.

"Good morning, little King," Feisal said, looking up from his book.

"Good morning." Federigo went over to the desk and peered at the manuscript Feisal was copying; he had to stand on his toes to see over the edge of the desk. "What's that?"

"Aristotle," Feisal said. "A translation and commentary by Avicenna."

Federigo craned his neck. Dipping his pen into ink, Feisal copied out one line from the manuscript onto a fresh sheet of vellum. He concentrated so hard that he held his breath. Federigo loved to watch the long loops and curls of Arabic script appear like a tail behind the moving pen. He saw a word that he recognized and waited until Feisal had ended the line.

"Is it about medicine?"

Feisal nodded. "How did you know?"

"That word there, that means blood."

"It does." Feisal glanced quickly at him. "Who taught you to read Arabic, little King?"

"Oh, I just learned." Federigo folded his arms on the side of the desk and rested his chin on his hands. "Who is that for?"

"The Master Hakim Ayub ibn Tariq."

"Don't bother Feisal, Federigo," David ben Isaac called. He came out of the back room, smiling. "It's hard enough to get him to work as it is." He put one hand out and drew Federigo away from the desk. "By the One God, you're filthy. What happened to you?"

"I fell in the street." Federigo flapped his shirt to knock off some of the dust. "An ox nearly trampled me." Looking up at ben Isaac, he smiled, but the old man put one hand up to his beard and stared down, frowning slightly.

"Federigo, you really ought to be more careful." Abruptly he turned and went over to a table, on which

piles of bound manuscript stood waiting to be delivered. He was tall, with long, slim hands that moved lovingly over books; on his head he wore a silk skullcap. Federigo went after him, catching a glimpse of something odd on the table.

"What's this?" he said, picking up a long wooden rod with notches on it. Across the top was a short crossbar, carved with Arabic designs.

Ben Isaac looked over from the book he was inspecting. "That's an astrolabe. Sailors use it to find out where they are at sea."

"How?"

Ben Isaac closed the book carefully and turned. "You put the crossbar on the horizon, and count the notches up to the North Star, and that tells you how far north you are."

"It's beautiful." The wood felt smooth under his fingers; it was lacquered, and the carved designs were painted in. He balanced the astrolabe in his hand. "If it's just a tool, why make it so beautiful?"

Ben Isaac shrugged. "Because people like beautiful things around them. And things that are important to them they often take loving pains with, to make them pleasing."

"Like a crown."

Ben Isaac stroked his beard. "Yes. Like a crown. Or books."

"Whose is it?"

"It belongs to a sailor who came in here looking for maps. He left it as surety while he went to find money."

Federigo ran his thumb over the designs. "An Arab sailor."

"No, he was Genoese."

"A pirate? He must have stolen it from an Arab." In the

dim shop, with the rustle of Feisal's pen in his ears, he saw in his mind a fierce sea battle, the ships thrashing through the water, the groaning of the slaves at the oars, and the crack of sword on sword. His hand tightened around the astrolabe. "Someday I'll go sailing."

"Not if you aren't more careful." Ben Isaac touched his shoulder. "You're just a boy, Federigo. You could be hurt very easily."

"I'll be careful." He put the astrolabe down, but his eyes remained on it. It made him wistful to think of the places the wooden tool had been, the men who had handled it. Someday I will have an astrolabe too, he thought.

"It's all over Palermo that there's an envoy from the Pope in Al-Aziz," ben Isaac said.

Federigo nodded. "He's here to talk to Diepold. He brought me a letter from the Pope." That made him laugh, remembering the letter.

"An amusing letter?" Ben Isaac smiled. He was a Jew and the Pope meant nothing to him.

"Well, he always writes me lots of advice, like that I have to treat everybody with justice and honor and that I have to remember the dignity of a king." Federigo shook his head. "It's all useless advice—he doesn't know what it's like down here, everything he says makes no sense to me down here. He says I must learn to be a good Christian king."

"That certainly is good advice," ben Isaac said slowly, but Federigo could tell by his tone of voice that he didn't believe it. Federigo opened a book in front of him and stared at the script. It was in Hebrew, which he could not read.

"It's silly advice. You're Sicilian, and you're a Jew. Feisal is Sicilian and he's a Saracen. How can I be a good king to you if I am a Christian? I mean—" He frowned, staring at the meaningless letters. "I am a Christian, but I can't be a king just of Christians, I have to be a good Jewish king and a good Moslem king, too." Was that possible? He cast a quick glance up at ben Isaac.

The tall man was staring down at him with a peculiar look on his face. A smile twitched at the corners of his mouth. "Federigo, have you ever said that to anyone else?" he asked.

"No. I just now thought of it."

Ben Isaac took him by the sleeve and led him into a corner. "Federigo, if I were you, I wouldn't tell anybody that idea. Do you know what heresy is?"

"Yes. That's when you don't believe in God." Federigo sat down on a pile of leather.

"Not really. It's when you don't believe in the teachings of the religion you're supposed to belong to. It's against the teachings of your religion to believe what you just told me." Ben Isaac sat down on a low chair. "Do you know what happens to heretics?"

Federigo shrugged. "Some priest tells them to watch out or they'll go to hell."

Ben Isaac's face tightened. His beard seemed to bristle. "Heretics are burned alive, Federigo." His eyes looked off into the darkness of his shop. "I'm not trying to frighten you. I hope no one will ever be able to frighten you. What you said is right. A king of many different peoples has to be above any kind of prejudice."

"I'll have to think about it some more. I just thought of it when I said it, I'm not sure it's right yet."

"I think you'll decide that it's right." Ben Isaac smiled. "But just don't tell anybody. Keep it in your heart and use it to guide you, but don't tell anyone."

"That's ridiculous. If I act that way they'll all know I believe it." Federigo cocked his head to one side. "Won't they?"

"Not necessarily. People say one thing and do quite different things all the time. People believe what they are told, they're not always smart enough to understand what they see." The beard wrinkled around his smile. "It's hard to be a Jew in a Christian world, Federigo. It's even harder to be a just king."

"Now you sound like the Pope."

Ben Isaac put his head back and laughed. "Perhaps. Older people sometimes sound alike when they're talking to boys."

The door opened; a little man in a sailor's leather breeches came in. "Ben Isaac."

"Excuse me," ben Isaac said. He rose and went over to the sailor. "Well. And now you have the money?"

"Three tarens." The sailor took out a purse. While he and ben Isaac dickered mildly over the price of the maps, Federigo walked around the shop, looking at the books waiting to be bound, their pages sewn into fat sheaves, and the leather cut to bind them with. He thought, there are good kings in places not Christian, too. Then why does the Pope always tell me to pray and go to Mass so I'll be a good king? He put his hands on a book covered with gold leaf and bits of jewels. Some merchant had probably ordered it—some rich man with a big house and dozens of coats and shoes. Scuffing his feet on the floor, he went to the door of the shop. When he passed the sailor, he smelled the sweat and oil of the man's body.

"Good-by, Master," he called. "I'll come back soon."

Ben Isaac leaned out around the sailor, and the sailor turned his head to look. "Good-by, Federigo. Be careful," ben Isaac said.

So. Be careful meant not only to keep from being run over by oxen, it also meant to watch out that people didn't know what he thought. Federigo went out into the hot street. It was time to go beg something to eat, and to find his friends and play.

"Federigo," Durante shouted. He came racing down the street, dodging in and out of the women carrying home their groceries and laundry in baskets on their heads. "Federigo."

"Don't yell," Federigo said. "I'm not going anyplace, and I see you." He sat down with his back to the wall, grinning. "What's going on? You look as if you've been in a fight."

Durante skidded to a stop in front of him and strutted up and down, his hands on his hips. "I just beat that Davide until he yelled for his mother." His knuckles were bleeding, and on the left side of his face bruises showed. Federigo took a bite of the sausage he'd been eating.

"There's a pirate ship in the harbor. I saw one of the sailors in ben Isaac's shop. He was Genoese—I could tell by his accent."

Durante sat down beside him, his knees drawn up to his chest, and wrapped his arms around his legs. "Do you want to go follow them around and listen to them swear?" he asked.

"Maybe later. Have some sausage."

"Sure."

Federigo watched him take a huge bite of the sausage, peeling back the scrap of linen that it was wrapped in. Durante was two years older than Federigo, much taller, and dark, black-haired and black-eyed, the fiercest fighter in Palermo except for the sailors. His father was a carpenter; Durante was supposed to be learning how to work wood, but he spent most of his time begging, stealing and fighting. Federigo laughed, thinking of that.

"What's so funny?" Durante said, his mouth full of meat.

"Nothing. Let's go find Yusuf."

"Good."

They leaped up. Federigo stuffed the sausage inside his shirt and trotted down the street toward the bazaar. All the merchants had set up their wooden stalls in the Vucciria— long counters for their goods and awnings to shield them from the sun; the awnings fluttered in layers up and down the street, green and blue and yellow, red and white striped, bright orange and white. Around them, the women of Palermo thronged, haggling over prices and hunting through mounds of oranges and vegetables and loaves of bread for the freshest, the sweetest, the ripest of everything. Their voices rose like the twittering of birds. Federigo, sliding between them, heard Arabic and Italian, Hebrew and Greek, all the languages intertwining, sometimes all spoken together.

The bazaar pleased him immeasurably. Franciscus had taught him the history of Sicily—how, in the beginning, Phoenicians and Greeks had built their cities and temples on the island; and how later the Romans had conquered it from them, only to lose it again to the Greeks of Byzantium; and how the Greeks had given way to the Saracens, sailing over the sea in their fleet galleys to rob and murder and finally to settle on the island with the remnants of the Greeks, the Romans, the Phoenicians; and how after a long period of turmoil the Normans of France had come, drifting down through Italy in little groups, and seized control and made themselves kings in Sicily (but never quite defeating the Saracens, who still had fortresses in the mountains); and how, with Federigo's father the Emperor leading them, the Germans had ridden down to destroy the Norman kingdom and create one of their own. Federigo could see all this history in the faces of the people, and hear it in their voices and smell it on their bodies, because each cooked and ate his food in a distinctive way and that gave each of them a particular odor. He stopped to watch a litter sway by, borne by mules, and inside a merchant with the black skin and crisp hair of a Moor; he stood eying a tall woman with a shawl over her head who spoke Greek to the Sicilian whose fish she was buying.

"Yusuf," Durante bawled. "Over here."

Yusuf was braiding strips of leather together, sitting in between two booths, his eyes dreamy. When he heard Durante, he leaped up and started toward them, grinning.

"Did you hear about Moshe?"

Federigo and Durante crowded around him, their heads bent so they could talk in the hubbub of the bazaar.

Durante said, "No. What happened to Moshe?"

"He ran away from home and spent all night on one of the ships in the harbor. The sailors fed him and told him stories, and they were going to take him with them, but his father found him and took him home."

"Oh—" Federigo beat his fists on his thighs. "Why? Why didn't he let him go?"

Yusuf's mouth pulled into a sly smile. "Well, because he's Moshe's father. If you had a father, Federigo—"

Federigo straightened up. "Yes? Go on." His skin felt hot.

Lazily, Yusuf shrugged, and with his sandaled foot drew a circle in the dust of the street. "Well, you'll never know, will you? I mean, having a father is—"

Federigo hit him hard in the stomach. Yusuf staggered back, and Federigo charged him, his fists pumping. Suddenly Durante's hard thin body was in his way, thrusting them apart; Durante yelled, "Come on, quit it, both of you."

Stepping back, Federigo blew on his knuckles.

"Make him apologize."

Yusuf was struggling in Durante's grasp, his hair falling in his eyes; he yelped, in Arabic, "Let me go. I'll kill him, I'll break all his bones."

"You'll try," Federigo shouted, dancing with rage.

Durante whirled and knocked Federigo away with one arm.

"You can't, Yusuf. He's the King."

Federigo lost his balance and sat down hard. The people around them were watching, some laughing, others shaking their heads and scowling. Getting up, Federigo started back toward Yusuf, but he'd regained his temper. He felt a little silly. Yusuf was right, he was an orphan, and it was stupid to fight over the truth. Yusuf was clawing his way out of Durante's grip.

"Let him go," Federigo said. "Yusuf, I'm sorry. I

shouldn't have hit you."

Durante said, "He shouldn't have teased you."

Yusuf wiped his mouth on his sleeve. "Just because you're the King—"

Federigo fisted both hands and charged in again. Durante yelped. For an instant, Federigo saw nothing but a whirl of Yusuf's cloth and face and the dusty street; his fists pounded on flesh, and something hard smacked into his eye. He shouted. Arms wrapped around his body, and he clutched Yusuf and tried to fling him down. Yusuf kicked him hard in the leg. Wrenching one arm free, he slugged Yusuf in the side, and the other boy fell.

"Stop," Durante said coolly. He grabbed Federigo by the arm and pulled him back. "Don't fight him when he's down."

"Why not?"

"It isn't particularly nice. Yusuf, get up and stop fighting, he can beat you."

Yusuf was sitting in the dirt, braced up on his arms, and his nose was dribbling blood. Slowly, one leg at a time, he got to his feet and straightened. His thin face looked murderous.

"Shake hands," Durante said. "Be friends again."

Federigo said, "If he stops teasing me."

"It's the truth," Yusuf muttered.

"Be quiet," Durante shouted, "or I'll beat up both of you, and you know I can do it, too. Go on, shake hands." He gave them each a shove.

Yusuf's hand moved out, the fingers spread, and cautiously Federigo took it and shook it once, hard.

"All right," Durante said. "Now let's go find some sailors

and listen to them swear."

They started off through the bazaar again. Yusuf kept looking threateningly at Federigo, whose eye was beginning to hurt. He put one hand up to it. Fighting was stupid, it only got him into trouble. He was going to have a black eye and Diepold would beat him. He felt unsure and unhappy and a little sick to his stomach.

"I'll have to show you some tricks," Durante murmured. "You'll be a good fighter one of these days, you aren't afraid of anything."

"All right," Federigo said. The idea of being able to do what Durante had done—stop them fighting just by a simple threat—interested him. But the thought of facing Diepold with a black eye made him glum. He couldn't fight or threaten Diepold. What good was knowing how?

"My children," Hakim Ayub said, lifting one hand. "A certain Kurdish shepherd had a number of sheep. Nearby lived his brother, who had sheep to the number of three times that of the first shepherd. Beyond a small river lived a third man, whose sheep numbered as many as those of the first two combined."

Federigo grinned. Hakim Ayub always made arithmetic problems into stories. Lifting one hand, Hakim Ayub glanced around the semi-circle of Saracen boys squatting before him on the floor and cleared his throat.

"My children, the sheep of the three herdsmen together attain a number which, when doubled, is one less than the square of the most sacred number. Tell me, my children, how many sheep each shepherd had."

Eight Saracen boys bent over their abacuses and writing

tablets. Federigo, who was leaning in the window, swung his feet slowly off the ground, balancing himself on his stomach on the windowsill. The most sacred number was nine, which was eighty-one squared, minus one—"

"Master," one of the Saracens called, and instantly the others began to shout, "Master, Master," and wave their hands for his attention. In his head, Federigo hastily divided forty by eight.

"Perhaps Federigo knows," Hakim Ayub said, in his placid voice. "Federigo."

"Five, fifteen and forty. I mean twenty." Federigo tilted forward over the windowsill and did a slow somersault to the floor of the room. They'd all beaten him. It was a disgrace to be asked for the answer. Hakim Ayub always asked the last to shout that he had it. And he'd gotten it wrong, a little. He sat up, cross-legged, and looked glumly at Hakim Ayub.

"Correct," the old Moslem said. "Did everyone reach the numbers five, fifteen and twenty?"

Of course they all had.

"Ummm. My children, the hour grows late, it will soon be the moment for prayer. You'll all have to run to reach your homes and the mosque. Dismissed."

The eight Saracen boys leaped up and raced screaming out of the room. Hakim Ayub winced and turned his dark eyes on Federigo. He had a wonderful face, seamed and wrinkled, the eyes buried in the pouches of his eyelids, and a small mouth always pursed inside a curly white wreath of beard. He reminded Federigo of a picture he'd once seen of Charlemagne.

"Well, Federigo," Hakim Ayub said, and shut his book. "You were slow on that last problem, my child. Don't you enjoy algebra anymore?"

"You misled me when you started talking about Kurds, Master. I was thinking of Jerusalem."

"A worthy subject for contemplation." Hakim Ayub picked up a pole and went to put the counters straight on his giant abacus. "I mentioned your lapse only because it astonished me. You're usually so quick. Your eye is lovely. What happened to it?"

Federigo made a face; that hurt his black eye, and he put his fingertips to it, feeling the swollen, sensitive lid. He could barely open it. It felt bruised, as if he could see the purple-black through his fingers.

"I got in a fight with Yusuf ibn Caidi."

Hakim Ayub frowned. Leaning his pole up against the cracked plaster wall, he said, "A difficult, wild boy, Yusuf. He was a student of mine for a while. And he's friendly with that Durante, too—that little . . . umh . . . little . . ." He stroked his cheek. "You shouldn't play with them, Federigo."

"They aren't bad, Master. I like them." It made him angry when Hakim Ayub tried to tell him what to do, and he shifted to get his legs under him.

"Most of the boys in my class begin shouting as soon as they hear someone else," Hakim Ayub said. "Whether they have the answer or not."

"That's cheating." Federigo wandered to the door, through which he saw the quiet garden just inside the Master's gate—the shadows stretched across the wall. It was getting late. "I may fight a lot and have bad friends, Master, but I don't cheat." He grinned at Hakim Ayub, who shut his eyes entirely, smiled, and nodded.

"Especially since you're clever enough to get the right answers most of the time, Federigo."

For a moment, going out into the garden, Federigo didn't understand what he'd said. With his hand on the wooden gate, he paused. That was odd. It sounded as if Hakim Ayub were saying that he didn't cheat because everything was easy enough that he didn't have to. He walked up the street, running his hand along the wall. That wasn't a compliment, no, it certainly was not.

The sun was going down. In the tall pine trees that filled the park around Al-Aziz, the wind moaned and cried like a baby. Someone once had told him that the sound of the wind was the voices of ghosts risen to prowl around at night. He quickened his steps, and all along his spine the hair stood on end. When he moved out from between the last of the houses on the street, and the street became the road to Al-Aziz, he felt the bite of the wind like a blast of cold.

Behind him, the lower town was already dark. He turned to look back into it, at the flood of shadow creeping slowly up from the harbor like an ocean drowning everything, houses, fountains, gardens and dogs. Off beyond the red-tiled rooftops, the spire of a minaret gleamed in the last level rays of the sun. There was something strange about it. Palermo at night was a different city, people were robbed and murdered, people went into alleys and never came out again. He thought he could see it changing before him, all the buildings crouching down to shield the thieves and killers in the dark. With a yelp, he turned and raced toward the palace. Sometimes being King of Sicily was nothing compared to being twelve and a good way from the light and warmth of home.

T HE LIGHT of tall candles played over the mosaics on the wall of the chapel—Mary on a white mule entering Bethlehem, the Coming of the Wise Men. Federigo clasped his hands behind his back, wishing the service were over. Franciscus had lectured him about his black eye all the way over from their part of the palace. Diepold so far had maintained an ominous silence. And Federigo had seen the Papal Legate gasp and make an exaggerated face when he'd first entered the chapel.

Now, at the altar, the Legate was reciting the last of the Evening Service, and all around Federigo arms rose and moved in the Sign of the Cross. In loud voices, they said the last prayer; and the Legate turned and blessed them, saying, "Go, it is complete."

"Amen," everyone said, loudly, and with Diepold beside him, Federigo turned and walked down the aisle toward the door, with all the other people standing at attention on either side. Halfway to the door, he felt Diepold's strong fingers grip his arm, and he gulped. It must be worse than usual to come home with a black eye when the Papal Legate was there. He quickened his steps, but Diepold kept up with him, of course. In fact, by the time they had reached the threshold, Diepold was practically dragging him. With a twist of his arm, Diepold wheeled him around the corner and into a quiet part of the courtyard.

"What happened to you?" Diepold hunkered in front of him and grabbed him by the shoulders. "Where did you pick up that eye?"

"I was born with it," Federigo said, angry. "It just changes color now and then."

Diepold shook him hard, so that his head snapped back and his neck hurt. "Don't talk back to me. Go to your room. I'll teach you not to fight like a common street brat. Go." He shoved Federigo toward the open courtyard and stood up, and Federigo with one glance at Diepold's tight red face broke into a run for the outer staircase. This, he could tell, was not going to be a regular beating, in which the louder he yelled the less it hurt. Franciscus was waiting for him halfway up the stairs and caught him by the arms.

"Oh, Federigo. Didn't I tell you it was a mistake?"

"At least he could have asked if I'd won the fight." But acting calm didn't help. He pulled Franciscus up the steps toward the second story door. Down in the courtyard, Diepold was talking to the Papal Legate, who kept twisting his neck to stare up at Federigo on the stairs. Federigo slipped inside the door.

"I'm going to run away."

"You what?" Franciscus wheeled toward him. "Federigo. An ordinary boy might be able to run away at will, but you are the King."

"Oh, not forever, just for tonight. Anyhow, I was going to go meet Durante and Yusuf in the park. He can't beat me twice, so it doesn't matter." He realized he was making little sense and shrugged.

Franciscus hauled him into their room. "You can't run away. If you disappear, it will upset everything—the whole kingdom. Don't you see that?"

"But I'm not going to disappear. You can tell him I'll be back in the morning." Federigo opened the closet and searched for his cloak. "They can beat me in the morning."

"They'll beat you twice as hard."

"And anyhow," Federigo said, pulling out the cloak, "he won't dare make a fuss, or the Legate would find out. Just tell him."

Franciscus snatched at him, and Federigo dashed for the door. "Tell him I'll be back in the morning." He slapped the door shut and ran for the far side of his wing of the palace. A page coming up from the kitchens dodged out of his way, startled. When he'd reached the little room just above the park, Federigo paused and looked out the window, looking for people around who might see him. There was no one. He rolled up the cloak and threw it out the window to the ground, swung himself out onto the ledge, and jumped down to the top of the wide, low wall below. From there, it was only a hop to the soft earth beneath the trees.

Looking up at the palace, he suddenly wished he'd stayed tamely to take the beating. Durante and Yusuf could have spent the night alone in the park—they did it often enough, when he couldn't get out. The pale stone of the palace gleamed in the moonlight, and a single star pricked the deep blue sky of the night. He gulped. It looked like a prison wall, locking him out in the world, away from home. He bent and picked up his cloak and jogged quietly off into the trees.

Just beyond the grove of trees, at the far end of the meadow where the tame deer grazed, stood a tiny pleasure house; and he headed for that. Beneath his feet the pine needles were slippery, and he had to keep his strides short. The wind moaned and sighed in the branches, a constant drone of noise. He stopped at the edge of the meadow and looked down toward the pleasure house. All the grass turned silver in the moonlight, and the wind made trails in it like an invisible animal running across the meadow. He was about to start across the open space toward the pleasure house when a hiss just behind him made him jump.

"Federigo," Durante whispered, and crawled out from under a bush. "Come here—there's someone in the pleasure house."

"Who?" Federigo sank down on his heels. Immediately Durante and Yusuf were beside him, their heads close together so they could whisper. Yusuf had on a Saracen head-cloth, but otherwise he was dressed like the other two, a shirt and loose trousers.

"I don't know who it is," Durante said. "We heard them talking when we came past. But they haven't got a lamp lit."

"Aha." Federigo peered toward the pleasure house. Obviously whoever was there didn't want anyone else to know about it. Just as obviously, that meant someone should. "Let's go down and find out."

Durante laughed. "I knew you would. Yusuf was scared."

"I wasn't scared—just smart." Yusuf belted Durante across the side with his arm.

"Well, keep quiet, don't let them see us."

Federigo on hands and knees raced out into the meadow. Halfway across to the next grove of trees, he flopped down on his belly, listening to the flurry in the grass behind him as Durante and Yusuf followed. When they landed next to him, he bounced up again and charged over the grass into the deep shadows under the cypress trees that crowded up to the rear wall of the pleasure house. With Yusuf and Durante pushing each other and muffling giggles, they darted from tree to tree, working down toward the little wooden shelter. An owl hooted in the meadow, and Federigo's hair stood on end. Staring out into the open, he saw a ghost of soft wings flapping into the shadows.

The door to the pleasure house opened, and a man's head stuck out. Inside, a voice said, "It's only an owl, you fool. Shut that door before someone sees you."

With a click, the door shut. Federigo crawled around a tree into the bushes against the wall of the house and crept along until he was directly beneath a window. Silent now, Yusuf and Durante glided after him, and they sat down cross-legged under the window, side by side.

Durante poked Federigo in the ribs with his elbow, jabbed his thumb toward the house, and cocked his eyebrows. Federigo shook his head. He recognized neither of the voices, which bewildered him—he knew everyone in Al-Aziz. Turning carefully around, he got to his knees and started to rise so he could look in through the window.

"It must be done before the Legate goes," the deeper of the two voices said. "Diepold will be able to cover it up otherwise."

Federigo froze.

"I wouldn't do it if I had a choice," the other voice whined. "You know I would not."

"Why? What's the difference about this killing, when you've killed so many?"

Beside Federigo, Durante jerked in alarm. Federigo's mouth had gone dry, and he was sweating, although the night was cool. I should not be hearing this, he thought.

"He is the last Hohenstaufen," the deeper voice went on. "He should never have been born—his mother was much too old to bear a firstborn child. Granted, it's a painful thing, to kill a child, but in the end, it will all come out for the better when he's dead."

Without his willing it, Federigo pushed himself away from the wall and raced back into the trees as fast as he could run. They were talking of killing him. The sudden darkness under the trees panicked him completely, and he crashed into tree trunks and stumbled over roots, fell and tore his skin on brambles, lurched up and ran on, his breath sobbing in his throat. He heard someone thundering after him, and his heart stopped. An instant later he ran into the wall.

"Little Red, it's me, it's Durante." Durante grabbed him by the shirt. "It's us, don't run."

"They want to kill me," Federigo said. Panting, he slackened his weight against the wall. The vines and bushes twined themselves around him, and branches scraped against the wall around his head. "They want me dead."

"We'll protect you," Yusuf said.

Durante hissed. "They heard us—they'll be looking for us. Let's go." He bent over, his hands on his knees. "Up over the wall."

Federigo's hands were shaking, and his knees wobbled. He glanced back toward the meadow. Now he knew why he hadn't recognized the voices—they had belonged to men either of the Legate's party or of Walter of Brienne's. Scrambling up onto Durante's back, he crouched and braced his hands against the wall. Yusuf, the lightest of them, climbed up on their backs and swung himself up onto the wall's wide top. Reaching down, he caught Federigo by the wrists and helped him squirm up beside him.

Durante backed off a little, looking up at the wall. Federigo stared back toward the meadow. In the trees, he could see something moving—a tame deer, perhaps, or an owl, but it could have been a man, too. He bent down, and when Durante ran straight to the wall and by momentum scurried halfway up it, he caught his wrists and hauled him up beside him.

"You're stronger than you look," Durante said, panting. "Come on, let's go someplace where we can think."

"The harbor," Federigo said. "Race."

They jumped off the wall into the street and ran down the slope toward the harbor, past the dark houses and shuttered shops that in the daytime looked so friendly. The dogs inside the gardens began to bark as they ran by, and the sound of their feet echoed in the narrow street. Federigo started to panic again. He couldn't keep himself from straining to go faster, to get away, and by the time they had reached the Street of the Doves he was nearly a block ahead of Durante and Yusuf. They were saving their strength. When he finally had to slow, with a stitch piercing his side and his breath burning in his lungs, they jogged up barely panting.

"Wait—wait just a minute." Federigo sank down against a building. "Let me—catch my breath."

They plopped down, one on either side of him. Yusuf said, "You can hide in Palermo until the Legate's gone."

Federigo shook his head. They might find him in Palermo —too many people knew him by sight. The air over his head was scented heavily with jasmine; there was a garden beyond this wall. He thought, I could go to Diepold and tell him what I heard. . . . But he might not believe me, and even if he did, he might not be able to protect me. The idea of letting someone else take charge of his safety made his throat close up with fear.

A black dog trotted out of the alley across from them, sniffed at them, and turned down toward the harbor. Federigo got to his feet. "Let's go—I don't feel safe up here."

Durante said quietly, "There's no place in Palermo that's safe."

"Where should I go?"

Striding along beside him, the bigger boy shrugged. "I don't know."

Yusuf said, "Stay in Palermo—we can find places for you to hide."

"No."

"You're just frightened. Palermo isn't bad."

"It's not you they're trying to kill." Federigo glared at him. They cut through a square with a fountain in the middle, stopped to drink, and went on down an alleyway full of garbage and fighting cats. Furry bodies fled at their approach. Federigo caught a whiff of the smell of the harbor, and with it he caught an idea.

"How did Moshe get on board the ship that night?"

"With the sailors." Durante glanced over at him and grinned. "Do you want to try to stow away?"

Federigo tossed his hair back over his shoulders. "As long as I have to leave Palermo, I may as well make it an adventure."

"Take us with you," Yusuf said. "We'll help you."

Durante laughed and did a little dance. "Oh, yes—we could all be pirates—"

"Well, we have to find a ship that isn't going too far away," Federigo said hastily. They turned a corner and were on the wide street that ran along the quays. All up and down it, lamps burned in the taverns, and the wash and roar of sound poured along the cobblestones—sailors fighting, singing, gambling and telling stories and drinking. Off on the bay, the ships bobbed in rows, their painted prows aimed to the east. Federigo yelped happily. This was one of his favorite places. In twos and threes, alone and in crowds, pirates and common seamen strolled along beside the water, laughing in explosions of sound, and throwing bottles against the buildings so that they broke.

"Let's go into the Black Rose," Yusuf said. "That's where Hadji-Mustafa's crew is staying."

Durante whistled in approval. They climbed up over an iron railing onto the steps leading to the Black Rose.

Federigo said, "Who is Hadji-Mustafa?" The name was familiar, but he couldn't remember— In the doorway of the tavern, he paused, amazed.

The Black Rose was packed with Saracen sailors. They'd heated up the room until it steamed, many of them were dancing, and others were banging away on tall painted drums, swaying back and forth. A huge bowl, as wide as Federigo was tall, stood in the midst of a mob of sailors who were dipping their cups into it; and the room stank of raw red wine. Yusuf and Durante dragged him into a corner, and they sat on the sawdust, staring open-mouthed at the men playing like children under the glaring light of the oil lamps.

Three sailors were dicing on the floor near them; one peered at them, muttered something, and slapped his hands together. The dice rolled across the uneven boards and bounced against a little sawdust wall. One of the three roared so loud Federigo clapped his hands over his ears, and silver coins flashed in the light. Oil and sweat shimmered on the sailors' broad, muscled shoulders.

There was a tremendous splash, and suddenly everybody was laughing. Federigo craned his neck to see around the bodies in his way. Someone had fallen into the bowl of wine. Dripping and sleek, he stood up, howling, and plunged off across the room.

"Moslems aren't supposed to drink wine," Federigo said to Yusuf. "Are they?"

Yusuf shrugged. "They say that Allah doesn't see what happens in Palermo. There's so much wrong with it that He gave up watching a long time ago. Look! There's Hadji-Mustafa."

Through the smoky, stinking room came a tall, slender man with bright gold hair. At first Federigo couldn't believe that he was Hadji-Mustafa—but the way the sailors

bowed to him and watched him told him that he must be. The blond man swung toward him, and he saw the neat red silk patch sewn over the man's right eye; and suddenly he remembered who this was: the greatest pirate in the Mediterranean. His heart leaped. Hadji-Mustafa had been born Christian, somewhere in the North; he'd been captured and made a galley slave, converted to Islam, stolen a galley from his masters, and collected a crew in every pirate's den in the world. Nobody knew how he'd lost his eye; everybody knew his ship; and everybody was afraid of him. Federigo stood up to see him better.

Hadji-Mustafa saw him at once and frowned. Murmuring, Durante reached up to pull Federigo down out of his sight. But the blond man only stared sharply at Federigo a moment and turned away, shrugging.

"Do you need cabin boys, Malik?" a sailor bawled, in Arabic. "There are three just begging to turn pirate." He laughed and shoved Yusuf roughly. "Aren't you? All three of you, dying to go out and fight great glorious battles on the sea."

"Yes," Yusuf shouted, and all the sailors laughed and rolled around, holding their sides. The men with the drums beat out a heavy tattoo.

"Not this time," the sailor said. "Maybe when we come back from Cairo, yes."

Federigo bit his lips. He'd been hoping the pirates would be sailing on to another port in Sicily, that they'd take him along. He didn't want to leave Sicily; he might never be able to get back. Sitting down again, he watched three sailors dance like great half-naked bears, their big feet thumping on the floor.

Durante pushed him. "Listen—over there."

Federigo looked. Hadji-Mustafa was counting out coins into a leather sack, while a big Moor bent over him talking; the pirate nodded every once in a while. Federigo could hear just a little of what they said—something about a fleet moving down from Genoa, heavily-laden and well-guarded. "But if a storm comes up, who knows? One of the merchants might be separated from the war ships." His eyes on the spill of gold running from his fingers into the sack, the pirate nodded and said nothing.

Yusuf whispered, "I wish we had some money."

Durante snorted and stretched his arms over his head. "What would you buy? They'd only steal it from you. I'm hungry."

Federigo shut his eyes. He imagined the Genoese ships rowing over the sea, and a storm boiling up, and one losing its way; the dawn would come and find that one ship alone, except for a pirate racing out of the distance, men in the shrouds waving their swords and lances. He gulped, longing to be on that ship. He thought, I could be a pirate, forget about Sicily and be a pirate. But he had been born to be King of Sicily. He sighed.

Durante was on his feet. Strutting a little, swinging his arms, he walked casually across the room, past the dancing sailors and the men bent over their throbbing drums, and stopped at the door into the kitchen. Yusuf whispered, "He's mad. They'll only kick us out."

"Maybe." Federigo got up. "Come on." He started after Durante, dodging around sailors who lifted cups full of wine and laughed and swatted each other with their great hams of hands. Halfway through the kitchen door, Durante was cajoling someone out of sight.

Abruptly a hand caught Federigo by the arm and swung him around. He twisted hard to get away, but the strong fingers tightened and held him—and Hadji-Mustafa bent to stare at him. "Who are you?"

Federigo swiped his hair out of his face. "One-eyed, like you, Master." He touched his black eye.

The big Moor behind the pirate laughed, but Hadji-Mustafa frowned.

"I think you're the King—this crowned child they're all so fond of. Don't you know they're looking for you all through the city?"

"What?" His heart sank, and he pulled at his arm in Hadji-Mustafa's grasp. Now they'd take him back to the palace.

"They're hunting you up and down Palermo." Hadji-Mustafa cocked his head to one side. "Maybe I ought to hold you to ransom, hah? Go on, go home, boy."

"I can't." Federigo searched for a way to ask; he could find none, but suddenly it burst out of him. "Take me to Cefalu."

"What?"

The Moor said, "He talks like a king, at least."

"Take me to Cefalu," Federigo said. "Or anywhere else on the coast of Sicily."

The sailors were packed around him, staring; one of them muttered, "He's a little mad, maybe." Yusuf was caught in their midst, and he whined.

"They're trying to kill me," Federigo said. "I have to hide for a while."

Hadji-Mustafa smiled faintly. "Hide in Palermo. Why

should I get mixed up in the government of Sicily?"

Federigo grabbed him by the robes. "Because I'm an orphan, and God says you should take care of orphans."

"I don't believe in your God anymore." Hadji-Mustafa started to stand up. "Go on home, boy. If you had a bad dream—"

"It wasn't a bad dream." Federigo hung on him, holding him down. "Take me to Cefalu." His blood was full of wild urgency, of an impatient wanting. "It doesn't matter which God you believe in, they all say that you must care for orphans."

"Oh, a sea lawyer." The blond man carefully disengaged Federigo's fingers from his clothes. "I wasn't planning to go to Cefalu."

"Anywhere, then. Anywhere still in Sicily."

"Naples, perhaps?"

The sailors roared with laughter, and Hadji-Mustafa grinned a little wider. He had a pleasant smile, but the stare of his one eye was fierce and direct, he never seemed to blink. In the lamplight his fair hair shone like silk.

"I'm afraid there are few ports where I can safely go in Sicily, little one," he said. "Find yourself another ship."

Federigo said, "You are a King, like me—what other ship is worth my sailing on?"

Now they were all howling, whooping with laughter and interest.

Hadji-Mustafa looked quickly all around. In the middle of the mob, Durante was yelling, and the sailors made a little way for him so he could reach Federigo's side.

"Take me, too," Durante said. "I won't miss this one."

"Oh, ho, so there's more of you. Am I to sail with half

the boy-population of Palermo hanging off my stern?"
Hadji-Mustafa took a cup from one of the sailors and drank
wine from it. His eye sparkled and flashed with laughter.
"Take you to Cefalu, eh?"

Federigo had said Cefalu only because it was one of the
few ports in Sicily he knew to be open to pirates; he
nodded.

"And what do I get in return?"

"When I really am King, I won't hang you."

The uproar doubled. The big Moor said softly, "He
knows how to talk to you, Malik."

Looking thoughtful, Hadji-Mustafa scratched his nose.
"So I see."

Federigo grinned. "I won't be any trouble, Master. I
don't even eat much."

"I wasn't planning to go to Cefalu."

"What good is there in being a pirate if you have to do
everything by plan?" Federigo hopped up and down with
impatience. "Please, Master, please. They really will kill me
if they find me. If I try to walk to Cefalu, someone will
recognize me and take me back to them."

Durante said, "He's telling the truth, Malik—I heard
them say what they meant to do to him."

"Who is this who wants to murder a child?" the Moor
said.

"People who want to rule the child's kingdom," Hadji-
Mustafa said. He reached out suddenly and grabbed a hand-
ful of Federigo's red hair. "I'm sick of black hair, I've had
nothing around me but hair black as the Pit for twenty
years. Yes, King, I'll take you to Cefalu."

The approving roar clogged up Federigo's ears, and he

grabbed Hadji-Mustafa's hand and kissed it. "I'll work, I'll help you. You can teach me how to sail."

Hadji-Mustafa stood up. "Hah. That I'll have to see." Raising his voice to a bellow, he shouted, "Abdul, when can we sail?"

"On the midnight tide," a deep voice roared.

Yusuf and Durante flung themselves on Federigo, hugging him. "You did it," Durante screamed. "You got us onto a pirate ship. You did it, Little Red!"

Federigo laughed and shivered both at once. He wasn't sure he trusted Hadji-Mustafa. No pirate could be trusted. But at least he was safe from the men in Al-Aziz. With the sailors rollicking around him, the noise shrieking in his ears, he thought of sailing, of going somewhere on his own, and abruptly his whole body sang with joy. This time he would have something to say about what happened to him. He felt fluttery all over with excitement.

N OW, HEAVE!"

Yusuf, Durante and Federigo flung their weight against the capstan bar—the three big sailors on the bar opposite theirs started to laugh, and Abdul, the first mate, glowered at them. They leaned into the capstan, and it began to turn, winding up the anchor rope. Federigo wanted to shout. Pushing as hard as he could, he put his head down and strained his shoulder muscles. Yusuf gasped for breath. The capstan turned slowly at first, but gradually it picked up speed, and shoving it around was easier. The rope turned wet and slimy.

"Out oars," Abdul shouted, his hands cupped around his mouth. "All right on the anchor, she's up."

Federigo stood back, panting. Through the holes in the sides of the ship, the oars flashed, dipped into the dark water of the bay, and thrust the ship forward.

Durante whispered, "We're going, we're really going," and flung his arm around Federigo's shoulders. "Look!"

Across the water, the lights of the harbor showed, reflected in streaks on the waves. On each boat anchored in the bay shone another light.

Federigo said, "Look—look at it all." He was bursting with excitement; he tried to hear and see everything at once, afraid of missing some detail.

Beneath their feet, the deck tilted slightly—they were under way. The oars groaned in the oar locks, and the water gurgled past the hull—the wind touched his face and cooled it.

Abdul shouted, "Sing out, watch." He spoke a mixture of Arabic and Italian and Greek, the universal language of the Mediterranean.

"Open water dead ahead," called the watch on the masthead. Federigo could barely see him, up above the yard with the sail wrapped tightly around it. The sailors in the hull, pulling on the oars, began to sing in deep, measured voices, fitting the rhythm of the song to the beat of the oars, boomed out on a drum.

"Make fast," Hadji-Mustafa said quietly, up on the stern near the tiller, and Abdul shouted, "Make fast." Halfway down the length of the ship, in the waist, a man leaning on the rail yelled it on up to the bow. Federigo looked around, wondering what they should do.

"Make fast," Abdul said, "means that if you find any rope loose, you wrap it around a cleat, like this." He nudged a piece of wood on the deck with his foot. "Or if you find anything rolling around loose, you secure it. Go on, make yourselves useful."

The three boys jogged off down the deck. The hull was completely open except for a narrow walkway on either side. In the middle, the oarsmen sat on benches, bracing their feet against the planking and heaving their weight against the oars. It looked like much harder work than Federigo ever wanted to try. He found a bit of rope trailing over the side and looked to see what it was attached to; it ran up into the shrouds that held the mast and yardarm in place. Groping on the deck, he found a cleat and wrapped the rope carefully around it.

"Not like that," the man in the waist said. "Here." He knelt, undid the rope end, and formed it into a figure eight. Slipping each loop over opposite ends of the cleat, he pulled it tight. "That way we can get it loose easily when we want to."

"Thank you." Federigo tried to memorize how he'd done it. Yusuf and Durante were already up to the bow, and he ran after them.

"Look," Durante said. He leaned over the railing around the bow and pointed down. Federigo pulled himself up on his stomach across the railing—at the foot of the prow the water churned up white, glowing.

"How far down do you think that is?"

"Oh, not far," Yusuf said.

Durante grabbed Federigo by the waist. "Can you swim?"

"Yes. Let me go." Federigo wiggled, and Durante pretended to push him over the rail. Yelping, they wrestled a moment.

"Quit that," said the sailor in the bow. "Don't make any fuss or you really will get pitched over. The Captain doesn't like fuss."

"Yes, sir," Durante said, soberly, and then giggled.

"Come on," Federigo said. "Let's explore."

"Oh, no, you don't," the sailor said. "Captain wants you below. Down there." He waved his arms back toward the stern, answering some signal.

"Down where?" Federigo said, doubtfully. He peered into the hollow the sailor had indicated. It looked like nothing more than a tiny cave made by the sides of the ship coming together into the point of the bow.

"Go on, that's where you'll be sleeping." The sailor pushed him.

"But can't we—"

"No! He says go below."

Federigo sighed. With his hands outstretched before him, he crawled into the dark, narrow space ahead of him. To his surprise, it was almost a room, large enough to stand up in, and full of folded canvas and huge coils of rope. Yusuf stumbled over something that clanked and sat down with a howl, holding his shin.

"Ssssh," Durante said. "Let's not get thrown off before we leave the harbor." He picked up what Yusuf had tripped over; in the dim light Federigo saw that it was a lantern. "I'm still hungry. We never did get fed."

"Do you think he'll really take us to Cefalu?" Yusuf asked. He sprawled out on the coil of rope behind him. "Maybe they'll take us to Cairo and sell us in the slave market."

Durante put his chin in his fists. "Maybe they'll hold you for ransom, Federigo. He did say something about that."

"Well, if he does, he won't get much." Federigo pulled at the canvas until it was spread out across the deck and lay down on it. "We should have brought something to eat."

Yusuf muttered something under his breath.

"What?" Durante said.

"I want to go home. My mother will be worried."

"So? Let them worry, it will do them good."

"But I miss them," Yusuf wailed. "I want to go home." He glared at Federigo. "You got us into this."

Federigo snuggled down with his head on his arms. "You could have stayed behind if you'd wanted to." He wished Yusuf would shut up. The thought of Franciscus, his own bed, a cherry jam tart before he went to sleep, all came unwanted into his mind and made him feel a little queasy. Franciscus would look for him in the morning and he wouldn't be there. They'd worry. Diepold would probably get into just as much trouble as if Federigo had actually been murdered. But that was Diepold's concern, not his. He just wished that his insides would stop turning over and that the lump in his throat would go away. Outside, the gulls cried and the rhythmic creak and splash of the oars mixed with the slap-slap of water against the hull of the ship. He felt very little and far from home, and getting farther away with each long stroke of the pirates' oars. Footsteps came up toward their cave.

"Is anybody in there hungry?" a strange voice whispered.

"Yes!" All three of them sat up.

"That's what the Captain thought." A round bundle rolled into the cave and stopped near Durante's feet. "He says if you get homesick, seasick or whatever, he's on watch all night long, but don't bother him unless it's serious."

Durante was already tearing off the wrapping on the loaf of bread.

"Thank you," Federigo called. "Hey, Durante, save some for us."

"Here." Durante tore off a chunk of the bread and tossed it to Federigo. "Yusuf?"

"I'm not hungry," Yusuf said, in a shaky voice.

"Oh, well, more for us."

Federigo chewed on a huge mouthful of bread. Whether running away was good or bad, it was done. With something in his stomach, he began to feel much better. The gentle rocking of the ship lulled him; when he'd stuffed himself with bread, he lay down, yawning, and listened to Yusuf sobbing quietly in the dark until he went to sleep.

When he woke up, it was still dark. Yusuf lay fast asleep on the coil of rope, but Durante was gone. Federigo crawled out onto the deck of the bow and looked around. The sail was stretched out on the wind; sailors dozed on the narrow walkway and the deck around his feet, and the oarsmen slept on their benches. He started aft, toward the stern, stepping carefully over the bodies of the sleepers in his way.

Overhead, the sky was moonless and covered with stars. He stopped, one hand on the rail, and looked up, amazed. Beyond counting, the stars swept across the sky, wheeling with the slow motion of the ship, so many of them he could barely pick out even the most familiar constellations among them. The broad sash of the Milky Way seemed as bright as the moon.

When he was closer to the stern, he could hear Hadji-Mustafa's voice, soft and pleasant: "That's called the Reaper's Star, where I was born, but the Arabs call it Razal-Gul, the head of the demon. The one over there, that looks red—hello, King."

"Hello, Master." Federigo climbed up the little ladder to the stern deck and sat down next to Durante. Hadji-Mustafa had the tiller bar in one hand. He was leaning up against the railing, his eyes on the sky and the sail.

"And the red star?" Durante said.

"That's called Sirius by the Christians—the Dog Star— but the Arabs call it The Red Eye. It shines brightest in the summer, when it's hot. King, that star up there, that's the Pole Star, as I was telling Durante. If you're ever lost that tells you which way is north."

"Do you have an astrolabe?"

"No." Hadji-Mustafa laughed. "Should I?"

"Well, I saw one in a shop in Palermo that a Genoese sailor had."

"I don't need one. I can tell how far north I am just by looking, I've been a sailor so long."

Federigo leaned his back against the railing. "Don't you ever get lonely for the place where you were born?"

"Not really."

"You said you were tired of black hair," Durante said. He stretched his legs out and yawned.

"Oh, that, sometimes. For people who speak the language I was born speaking. But I'm a sailor, I'm never happy unless I'm on the sea. So I don't get homesick."

"Why are you a pirate?" Durante said. "Couldn't you be a sailor for someone else?"

Hadji-Mustafa laughed again, but this time it was harsh and hard to listen to. "And sail on someone else's ship? Not me. I could work my whole life away and never save

enough money to get my own ship, either. I'm a pirate because it's the only way I can do what I want. Otherwise I'd
spend my whole life waiting for the day when I could be
free, and when I died, why, I'd never have gotten there."

The two boys were silent. Federigo was thinking that
he'd always taken for granted that people became pirates to
get rich, to fight and steal and kill people. But what Hadji-
Mustafa had said made more sense to him. He listened to the
creak of the timbers in the ship and the swish of the water
past her hull.

"Is that why you changed your God?" Durante said.

"Yes. Otherwise I'd have been a slave all my life. And
they weren't paying very high for skinny Christians in the
slave auctions that year."

Federigo thought it made no difference anyway—all
gods were the same, only the religions differed.

"I even went to Mecca," Hadji-Mustafa said. "Because I
could sail there. Not all the way, most of the way."

He lifted his head. Federigo felt the hair on the back of
his neck prickle up. It was as if Hadji-Mustafa heard something, a voice speaking, that they couldn't hear; he listened
intently a moment and shifted the tiller. "Abdul!"

Down in the waist, Abdul got up and shouted back.

"Trim the sail!"

Abdul went around kicking sailors awake, and they
moved around loosening ropes and moving the sail around.
Hadji-Mustafa moved the tiller steadily to one side; Federigo could feel the ship heeling slightly over.

"How did you know to do that?" Durante asked.

"The wind. I felt it change."

Durante whistled. "Will you teach me how to do that?"

"No one can teach you, you have to learn the feel of the wind."

"How long will that take?"

"That depends on you. Some people never learn."

Federigo rested his head against the railing. Everything about sailing pleased him—the roll of the ship, the touch of the cool wind, the stars overhead, and, beyond the innumerable small noises, the great silence of the sea. When I am grown up, he thought, I'll have many ships. Beside him, Durante went on asking questions in a voice tight with a passion to know the answers by heart, to know them in his bones, the way Hadji-Mustafa knew them. Federigo listened only casually. The music and peace of the ship made him drowsy, and he sank into a half-dream, in which the sun-blasted plain of Palermo itself rose up to acclaim him King.

"Like that. Right, Durante. Let me see yours, Red. Good. Yusuf—" Abdul shook his head, took the spliced rope from Yusuf, and carefully picked it apart. "You're not a sailor, sonny, that's all."

"I don't want to be," Yusuf said, and wiped his nose on his sleeve. "I want to go home."

Federigo made a face at him. "We'll go home when we reach Cefalu. You'd better make the best of it. Show him, Abdul."

"I'm trying," Abdul said. His forehead ran with sweat, and his thick, curly hair stuck to his face. Nimble as a girl's, his big fingers braided together the two ends of the rope. "Now. See?"

"I guess so." Yusuf took the rope ends back and undid them. "When can we do something else?"

"I'm just teaching you so you can splice up all those sheets," Abdul said. "That's what the Captain said. He said as long as you were on board to put you to work."

Yusuf wailed. "How far is it to Cefalu?"

"Three more days."

Durante murmured, "That's too short." Already deft, like Abdul's, his hands put together another splice. Federigo concentrated on getting the right pieces together and woven tightly.

"When we get to Cefalu, what will we do?" Yusuf said.

"Go back home, probably," Federigo said. "The Legate will be gone by then."

"How?"

"I don't know. Maybe we—"

"Sail," the lookout shouted from the mast. "Red sail to windward!"

Federigo jumped up and ran to the rail. In the hull, the sailors were racing to their benches, and their excited voices boiled up to his ears. Far down the leaping, glittering water, a red scrap danced—the ship coming. He leaned over the rail and squinted to make it out.

"Get forward," Abdul shouted to him. He grabbed Yusuf and Durante by their shirts and tossed them up toward the bow. "That's a Genoese, that's an enemy. Go on, will you? Run!"

Durante whooped. "A battle. They're going to fight a battle." He jumped up onto the railing to see.

"Get those brats forward," Hadji-Mustafa roared. He was coming up on deck from his cabin below the stern. Federigo took one look at him and streaked for the bow, yelling to the others to follow.

The ship seethed with action. All the oarsmen had gotten to their benches, and with a thundering roll the drumbeat started up; the sail had been tucked around the yard. Abdul and three other men dragged a chest out onto the foredeck just as the three boys darted into the shelter of the bow. Tipping up the lid of the chest, Abdul reached in and pulled out a sword.

"She's coming down on us," the lookout screamed. "She's taken in her sail!"

"Hard to windward," Hadji-Mustafa shouted. "Abdul, get up here."

Federigo climbed into the rigging on the bow. Swinging their oars, the rowers turned the ship neatly into the wind. Federigo shaded his eyes. Now he could see the Genoese ship crawling on her oars down toward them. His hands began to sweat, and he dried them on his shirt. Off down the sea, on the opposite side from the Genoese ship, he could just catch a glimpse of the coast of Sicily, gray against the blue sky.

"Pull," Durante whispered. He was rapt, leaning forward over the rail, his eyes fastened on the other ship. Sailors leaped past them into the rigging, carrying a net aloft, and strung it across the prow of the ship.

"What's that for?"

"In case they try to board us," Durante said.

"What if we get killed?" Yusuf clutched Federigo. "What if they take us prisoner?"

"What if the sky falls on us and cracks our heads?" Durante said. "Oh, shut up."

Federigo cast a quick glance around the ship. All along her deck, sailors with swords and daggers were stationed, tense and ready. In the rigging men with bows were crawl-ing into position, wrapping their legs tight around the ropes that braced the mast. Hadji-Mustafa stood at the tiller, his long fair hair blowing in the wind.

"Can you make her out?" he shouted, and a man at the foot of the mast relayed the call to the lookout.

"Not yet, Malik."

"Double-time, Abdul."

The drum in the hold picked up a faster beat, and the oars swung to meet it, crashing and groaning in the oarlocks. With each stroke, the breath exploded from the lungs of the oarsmen; Federigo could hear it clearly. He jumped up and down, excited. Yusuf was praying in Arabic.

"I wish they'd give us swords," Durante said. "I wish they'd let us fight."

Federigo cried out wordlessly—the ship ahead of them was wheeling away. "They're running—look."

All over the ship, a roar of triumph went up. Abdul bel-lowed, "She's turned, Malik—she's seen who we are."

"Let's try to catch her," Hadji-Mustafa shouted.

Everybody cheered but Yusuf, who was praying as hard as he could, and Federigo. They could lose days chasing the Genoese ship—they could even go so far off course for Cefalu that Hadji-Mustafa wouldn't want to go there. He stared glumly after the Genoese. "Coward."

Abdul jogged up. "She's running for Cefalu. We'll catch her before then." He pulled a canvas sack out of the cave where the boys slept and trotted back toward the mast.

"To Cefalu," Federigo murmured. He narrowed his eyes, watching the Genoese ship. She still looked far away, but she was definitely heading for the coast, although on a

long tangent of a course. He wondered why Hadji-Mustafa was chasing her; the Genoese were pirates, too, especially the ships that traveled alone. He folded his arms on the rail and watched.

When he looked around again, Yusuf was huddled in the shadow of the railing, looking glum, but Durante was nowhere around. Finally Federigo saw him helping Abdul and another man fasten a strip of blue silk to a line. Abdul and the other sailor stepped back, and Durante, glowing with pride, ran the silk pennant up the mast. Federigo grinned. Durante would get himself involved in everything that went on—he was like that when he enjoyed something. He turned back to watch the Genoese ship.

All that day they crawled over the sea after the other vessel. Since they were running before the wind, Hadji-Mustafa had them put up the sail, and the oarsmen rested, talking and drinking at their benches. Durante went around with Abdul, asking the names and uses of all the equipment he saw—every bit of rope and projection of wood. Federigo watched the ship they were chasing, wondering how far away it was.

They were catching up, but the wind was dying—already, the sail of the other ship was fluttering loose, and the sea grew glassy calm between them. The Genoese put out its oars; and a moment later Hadji-Mustafa gave a shout, and Abdul passed it along, and the oars of the pirate ship rattled out and drove into the water. Federigo could see the men on the Genoese looking apprehensively back toward them; they began to throw barrels overboard to make their ship lighter.

All afternoon, the two ships rowed down the sea, with

Hadji-Mustafa's creeping steadily closer to the Genoese, like a pursuing demon. The grating of the oars in the oar-locks began to get on Federigo's nerves. He gritted his teeth, listening to the incessant rasp of wood on wood, and tried to think of something else. But he was fascinated by the chase; he watched the Genoese draw nearer, in spite of all they tried to do to get away from Hadji-Mustafa, and he felt sorry for them.

By sundown, he was feeling sorry for himself. Spending all day in the sun had given him a sunburn that made it hard to touch anything without crying out. And Durante was climbing all over the ship—Abdul and Hadji-Mustafa answered every question he asked. Federigo thought it wasn't fair, Durante had a father. He wished, as he had before, that his father was still alive: He imagined him very tall, and red-headed. The Emperor. He'd sit on the throne and teach him how to judge people and how to make laws, how to lead an army and how to fight. They'd go hunting together, his father and he—he'd have his own hawk, and his own horses, a whole stable of them. He'd always have lots of clean shirts and plenty to eat. His father and he would go places together, and when he was bad, his father would beat him and not send Lothair to do it. Federigo rubbed his eyes with his fists to grind out the tears and wondered what it was like to have a father. If you had one, obviously, you took it for granted. He couldn't even remember that anyone had ever told him that his father had seen him—all the while Federigo was a baby his father had been ruling and fighting in the south, and Federigo had been in a nursery in the north.

It was silly to brood over things he couldn't change. He

wandered back into the waist of the ship and found Durante cheerfully beating Abdul and a sailor named Oddi at dice; two or three other seamen stood around laughing and making jokes about it.

"You're bright red," Abdul said, when Federigo sat down beside Durante.

"I know. I can feel it." He touched his cheeks gently with his fingers and winced. His skin felt as if it were burning.

"The sun bounces off the sea," Oddi said, "and hits you harder. All right, little tiger, it's your cast."

Durante picked up the dice and shook them; his white teeth flashed in his face. He'd gotten tan. With a whoop, he cast the dice, and they rolled over and over, wobbled to a stop, and came up three fours. The sailors all groaned.

"How did he do that?"

"He's cheating."

"No, they're Oddi's dice."

Around Durante's feet, a collection of small coins and bits of jewelry and clothing lay.

Federigo picked up the dice. "Can I play?"

"You have nothing to bet," Durante said.

"Just once," Federigo said, and rolled the dice. They clattered on the deck and lay still. Abdul roared.

"It's Palermo. They all learn to throw dice from the age of six months." He stared at the dice. Federigo had rolled a thirteen. "I'm not gambling with any boys from Palermo ever again."

"On your feet," Hadji-Mustafa yelled. "She's coming about."

Federigo bounded to his feet. The Genoese ship had

swung around broadside to the wind, and her oars thrust out motionless from her sides. He said, "Are they going to fight?"

Abdul laughed. "No. They're surrendering. Look."

Durante swore a round sailor's oath. "I wanted to fight."

"Hunh. You would." Abdul swung around. "Lower out the boat. Oddi, Feisal, Marco, Yaya—"

Federigo trotted up to the bow. The Genoese ship rolled in the water, helpless, and on her stern her master was waving a white cloth slowly back and forth. It occurred to him that pirates didn't fight as much as he'd thought—not if they could help it. He watched the little boat put off from the ship and scull toward the Genoese, packed with men. Why fight if you would only lose, and maybe die? He wondered if they'd take the Genoese prisoner, or just rob her of her stores and whatever plunder she might have collected. All in all, he decided, being a pirate wasn't as exciting as the stories made it out to be.

The boat came back full of bales of cloth, barrels of salt meat and wine and bushels of grain; most of the men had stayed on board the Genoese. Federigo watched while the sailors under Hadji-Mustafa's direction packed the plunder into the hold. Once again, the boat went dancing over the waves to the Genoese. Waving their swords and shouting, the pirates jumped down into it and started back toward their own ship. From the Genoese ship came howls and hoots and insults, and the pirates shouted back, full of blood-chilling threats and promises.

Hadji-Mustafa came up beside Federigo. "You're good luck to me, King. They were carrying a lot of gold, on top of all the rest."

"Oh. Well, I'm glad it was worth your doing it."

"What's the matter, disappointed? No blood, no fire?"

Federigo shook his head. "I'm kind of glad about that. It's just that . . . I don't know. It doesn't seem all that much fun." He shrugged. "It just seems like what you were talking about last night—working all your life away for nothing." He cocked his head to one side. "I mean—what will they do—what will *you* do with that gold? You'll just spend it all as soon as you reach a port and have very little to show for it. Won't you?"

"You sound like an old man."

Federigo grinned. "All my teachers are old men, that's why."

"Well, you're right. About my crew, at least. But in the meantime I do as I please. I sail where I want to, and I have my own ship—that's all I want. I don't care about the gold, just about sailing." Hadji-Mustafa took a little pot from his shirt. "Here, put that on your sunburn."

"Thank you."

"It wouldn't bother me if I never robbed another ship," Hadji-Mustafa said. "So long as I—"

"Could do as you please," Federigo said. "That's a good reason, I guess."

"Thank you," Hadji-Mustafa said, with exaggerated politeness. He stared down at Federigo, and finally he shook his head. "Do you want to be King?"

Federigo nodded, unscrewing the top of the pot; he dipped out salve on his fingers and spread it on his face.

"Why? It's probably more trouble than piracy, and about as dangerous and hard on other people."

"So I can do as I please," Federigo said, and laughed. Hadji-Mustafa, surprised, laughed too, and thrust out his hand. Federigo wiped off the salve hastily and shook hands with the pirate.

"We understand each other," Hadji-Mustafa said. "Good. I thought so, back in Palermo. Come along, now, we have to eat."

THERE'S CEFALU," Hadji-Mustafa said. "Do you want to go ashore now, with me, or after we eat tonight?"

"Now," Yusuf said. "Please, Little Red, can we?"

Federigo nodded. "We have to find a way to go back home. We can't do that in the dark." He stared at the shore. The bare brown-green coastline turned to white sand at the sea's edge, then to white foam, and darkened gradually to a bright, clear blue. Fishing boats painted red and yellow sailed and rowed about the harbor. Palm trees sprouted above the beach, beneath the tremendous cliff, and right below the rock he could see the double spires of the Cathedral one of his ancestors had built. The rock was shaped roughly like a head, which was probably why the town was called Cefalu. He wished he knew what he was going to do when he got on the beach.

"Red," Durante said, "I'm not going."

Federigo swung around. "What do you mean?"

Durante was fairly dancing with happiness. "I'm staying

with the pirates."

"Oh." Suddenly Federigo had a lump in his throat. He couldn't imagine not being able to find Durante whenever he wanted someone to play with. But he understood why Durante wanted to stay on the ship. He remembered how eagerly Durante had asked Hadji-Mustafa questions about sailing, that night on the deck under the stars. He flung his arms around Durante and hugged him.

"Have a good time. Come see us when you put into Palermo."

"I will." Durante hugged him back. "Don't get killed. And learn how to fight."

"I will."

"And tell my father that I'm all right and happy, and that I've gone to sea." Durante glanced at Hadji-Mustafa, who was waiting impassively, the boat's cable in his hand. "Don't tell him that I've gone with the pirates, though."

"All right." Federigo watched Hadji-Mustafa grin sarcastically. Yusuf climbed over the rail and, clutching the rope, let himself down gently into the boat—as Abdul had said, he wasn't a sailor. Federigo took hold of the rope in both hands. He'd seen the sailors do this, and he wanted to try it. With one leg wrapped around the rope to keep him from going too fast, he slid down with a whoosh and a thump into the boat. Yusuf in the stern of the boat was laughing.

"I can hardly wait to step on the ground again. I'm so sick of ships I could die." He bounced up and down.

Hadji-Mustafa landed beside him and cast off. "Federigo, fend us off."

Standing awkwardly on the gunwale, Federigo pushed

them away from the ship. High above them, Durante was calling good-by.

"I like to sail," Federigo said. "Someday—"

Abruptly he realized that he was falling. He wobbled, flailing with his arms to get his balance again, but the boat seemed to drift quietly out from under him. He yelled. Beneath him was nothing but scummy water—he took a deep breath and shut his eyes and fell in. Warm as milk, the water closed over his head. He thrashed his way to the surface and looked around, flipping his hair out of his eyes.

Yusuf was rocking back and forth with laughter, and Hadji-Mustafa's grin had broadened enormously. From the rail of the ship, the shrieks of the sailors' mirth reached him.

"Wait for me," he yelled. Embarrassed, he struck out clumsily for the boat, which was gliding off over the waves.

Hadji-Mustafa raised the sail a little, took hold of the tiller, and sailed the boat down toward him. Federigo waited, treading water, and splashed Yusuf. "You be quiet. At least I can swim." Lunging forward, he caught the gunwale of the boat and heaved himself into it, falling into the bilge.

"You looked so funny," Yusuf said. "You looked so surprised."

"I was." Federigo laughed. "But it's nice—it's warm."

Durante shouted, "Good-by, Little Red," and Federigo turned and waved to him.

Hadji-Mustafa put the helm over, and the boat skimmed down toward the harbor, past the fishing boats trailing their nets.

"You'll dry out quickly enough."

Federigo took off his shirt and wrung it out over the

water. "Do you know if we can catch a ride with a caravan to Palermo?"

"Probably. The bazaar is in the square in front of the Cathedral—those spires there."

"I know—my great-grandfather built them." He spread out his shirt in the wind and flapped it.

"Be careful, though," Hadji-Mustafa said. "They'll probably be combing the island looking for you. Of course, if you get caught, you'll go straight back home."

Federigo shook his head. "I don't want to get caught."

Hadji-Mustafa put his head to one side. "You won't either, if I know you at all, and I think I do. Yusuf, get up in the bow and fend off from the quay."

"I don't know how," Yusuf said.

"Oh, you." Federigo scrambled past him and stood up in the bow. The quay swept up toward them—boys and men were fishing from it, their lines drooping down into the water. He leaned out and caught a piling and held the boat steady against it; the thrust of the sail nearly carried the boat out from under him again. Hadji-Mustafa lowered the sail. A man on the quay over Federigo's head threw down a thick, slimy rope, and Federigo made it fast to the bow of the boat.

"Up you go," Hadji-Mustafa said. He tossed Yusuf easily up onto the quay and swung himself up, his lean body twisting. Federigo used the rope to pull himself onto the flat planks of the wharf, in among the old fish heads and the glitter of scales. The whole quay stank of fish.

"Now," Hadji-Mustafa said. "If you go down that way and turn left, you come to the Cathedral." He glanced around at the people watching them curiously; strands of his long blond hair were caught across the silk patch on his eye. "Be careful, as I told you. And remember your promise."

"What was that, Master?" Federigo was putting on his shirt, already nearly dry.

"Don't hang me," Hadji-Mustafa roared, and laughing strode off down the quay, with the men darting respectfully out of his way.

Yusuf said, "I'd do that first thing, if I were you."

Federigo shrugged. "He'd be too hard to catch. Come on." At a trot, he headed through the mobs of people around the harbor, toward the spires of the Cathedral jutting up beneath the huge, head-shaped cliff.

"I wish Durante had come with us," Yusuf said. He stopped just long enough to snatch an orange off a stall while the vendor wasn't looking. "I'm going to miss him."

"He'll have fun, and maybe he'll get rich." In a square fringed with palm trees, Federigo paused to get his bearings. On one side of the square was a tavern, with horses tethered in front of it. He looked hard at one of the horses and pulled Yusuf into the shadows.

"What—"

"I know that horse—that's Lothair's horse. Come on!" He burst into a hard run, headed out of the square. Yusuf raced along beside him; they careened through a street lined with little shops and full of shoppers. Federigo ran into a fat man, who grunted and thrust him off, and cut down an alley into the next street.

"What will they do if they catch you?" Yusuf asked, panting. He looked around. "There's the Cathedral."

Federigo nodded. "I don't want to find out." He glanced

over his shoulder toward the square where he'd seen Lothair's horse. Hadji-Mustafa was right. They were searching the island for him, and he'd never have gotten this far if he hadn't been on a ship, out to sea. He jogged down a tiny street and out into the square before the Cathedral.

It looked something like the one in Palermo—he paid no more attention to it than that. The square itself teemed with people. On three sides, the merchants had set up stalls, and they stood beside them, shouting their wares into the crowd that billowed around buying. Federigo sidled over to a stall selling cheeses and leaned against it, whistling unconcernedly. A tall, gaunt woman in a black shawl started haggling with the vendor; and while the man was arguing prices, Federigo's hand shot out and closed over a wheel of yellow cheese. He stuck it inside his shirt and ambled away.

Yusuf was eating his orange. "You should have made Hadji-Mustafa give you some money. He said you brought him good luck."

"Not good enough to be paid for." Federigo edged closer to a stall filled with live chickens in boxes, with cuts of beef and slabs of mutton, and, most important, sausage. There were three men watching the stall; he waited until two were busy with customers and the third was trying to fasten the lid back on a crate of screeching chickens. A fat sausage joined the cheese in his shirt. Folding his arms over his chest to hide his loot, he drifted with Yusuf through the crowd, looking for a baker's stand.

"How are we going to find a caravan?" Yusuf asked. He'd finished the orange.

"Sssh."

The woman behind the racks of still-warm bread glared

at him, and he smiled at her as sweetly as he could. She made shooing motions to him and he backed off. Suddenly Yusuf was pulling at him, whispering, "Come away—look!"

Federigo glanced over—and saw two knights riding past, talking. He stood still, his breath stopped in his lungs. The knights kept on going, but one of their horses passed so close by that its tail swiped across Federigo's arm. He turned to run, saw that the woman in the stall was staring after the knights, and with a shrug thieved a loaf of bread. Keeping the knights in sight through the corner of his eye, he led Yusuf off into the shadow of an olive tree and sat down to eat.

"But how are we going to find a caravan?"

"Be quiet, will you? All in good time." He twisted off the end of the sausage, took a bite and chewed. "Is there a fountain here?"

"Across the way."

"Good." He took a bite of cheese and one of bread and chewed them together. "Here, have something to eat."

"I can't understand you when your mouth's full," Yusuf said, but he took the sausage and bread. They passed all three back and forth between them, until they were both full, and Federigo stuck the remains of everything inside his shirt. It was well past noon, and the crowd was thinning out. The knights were not in sight. Federigo hoped they'd given up the search, but it had only been a few days. It seemed like weeks. He trotted across the square to the fountain and drank away his thirst. His hair was so long it hung down in the water and got wet. That was the worst thing—anybody seeing him would remember his red hair long afterward; and if a knight asked, they'd tell. He looked around, frowning.

"When are we going to find a caravan?"

"Now. Be quiet."

Getting up, he ran at a long trot through the thinning crowds around the steps of the Cathedral; usually, the carts and people necessary for caravans gathered in the church-yards, or at least posted signs about their destination there. He waited while three women in mourning argued over who should go first into the church and followed them onto the raised piazza before the main entrance. A priest stood to one side conferring with an old man leaning on a staff; two boys in white robes were reciting parts of the Mass at each other. But over near the railing around the piazza a huge, old man was sitting in the late sun, fanning himself with a palm frond. That looked promising. Federigo went over and bowed.

"Hello, Master."

The man, whose face was so fat his eyes looked buried in the folds of his cheeks, opened one eye and nodded. Fede-rigo sat on his heels, trying to look respectful.

"Please, Master, will you help me?"

"What do you want, little boy?"

"Is there a caravan going to Palermo soon?"

The fat man stopped fanning himself, shifted his gigantic hams so that he was sitting more comfortably, and lifted the palm frond again. "To Messina, tomorrow. To Taormina, in seven days. To Palermo, yesterday."

"Yesterday."

"That is correct."

Federigo stared at him. The palm frond waved gently

back and forth, stirring the air lightly over his face. Behind all that fat, a tiny moist gleam revealed the big man's open eye. Federigo said, politely, "And can you tell me when yesterday, Master?"

"Late."

"And by which road?"

The palm frond paused again. A big horsefly buzzed in the air near the fat man's shoulder, ready to descend; abruptly one enormous hand heaved up and swatted the air, and the horsefly zoomed wildly off. "There is only one road to Palermo from Cefalu."

"Thank you, Master."

"You are welcome, little boy." The hidden eyes gleamed maliciously. "Hurry and go before someone notices you are redheaded and twelve."

Federigo started and nearly fell over. The fat man's mouth curved into a perfect half-moon of a smile, and deep inside all the fat a laugh bubbled. Federigo bowed again, this time with real reverence, and darted back down the steps toward Yusuf, waiting in the shade of the olive tree.

"We have to follow them and try to catch up. They left yesterday."

"Yesterday? But we'll never catch them."

"Oh, Yusuf, shut up. Come on, we have to hurry." Federigo dragged him to his feet. "They can't move fast, not with carts and everything else."

"But we don't even know what road—"

Federigo hissed between his teeth. Yusuf had proved a complete loss the whole trip. Tugging him along, he headed out the north side of the square, back into the town, and followed the farmers from the bazaar who headed west.

Empty carts rattled down all the streets, but most of them were going either west or east—Federigo knew that they'd all follow the main road. He kept close to a cart painted with the story of the Flight from Egypt, hiding behind it whenever they passed crowds.

The bells of the Cathedral began to ring, deep and booming, calling the people to the evening service. A window shutter banged open, and a woman shouted, "Giacopo? Giacopo, come home for dinner." Somewhere children were yelling and laughing. Federigo gritted his teeth. Feeling homesick would do no good. The dust stirred by the ox he followed got into his throat, and he hawked and spat, already thirsty again. Beside him, Yusuf started to complain again, but Federigo didn't listen. They passed the last houses of Cefalu, and he sniffed meat cooking, bread warm from ovens, and touched his shirt to make sure their supplies were still there. It was going to be a long walk if they couldn't find the caravan. He pulled off to the side of the road, out of the dust, and strode along toward the sun, sinking down below the rim of the hillsides before him.

The road descended to the beach and ran along it; in the gathering evening, the waves curled up phosphorescent, boomed lazily on down the shore, and hissed back into the sea. Gradually, the crowds from Cefalu turned off the road to go to their homes. By moonrise, the boys were alone on the road, which ran off curving below the cliffs, pale under the silver light of the moon. Federigo began to get hungry again.

"Do you want to—"

"Look!" Yusuf grabbed him and pointed.

Federigo whirled around. Far up the beach, a bonfire burned.

"Maybe it's the caravan," Yusuf said.

"I doubt it. They'd have come much farther than this." He glanced back the way they had come. "It might be bandits."

Federigo could see men crouched around the fire. Bandits, a caravan, whatever it was, he knew he didn't want to go down there. Something strong in him warned him away from it. He started off along the road again, his eyes on the fire. With all the landscape around it dark blue in the night, the fire made a red-yellow blot in the middle. As they drew even with it, he heard voices—the road followed the cliff up away from the sea, and the fire burned below them— and he saw horses tethered off to one side. Big horses. He leaned forward into the steep slope of the road, listening to the ring of muffled laughter from the beach below him. Horses that big meant knights. Whatever had warned him had been right. Even if they weren't Diepold's men, they'd be dangerous; they'd know him, and loose bands of knights got bored and amused themselves doing strange things, like teasing strangers. Or kidnapping runaway kings. He sat down suddenly by the side of the road, too tired to climb any higher.

"This road—"

"Ssssh." Federigo glanced down at the fire. It looked far off, but voices traveled at night. He looked up at the cliffs rising sheer above the road. If they could find a cave in there, or even a place where the cliff overhung the road, they could sleep safe in case of rain. He got up again, feeling the muscles of his legs start to ache, and walked along

watching the cliff. Yusuf shambled along behind him, whining every few steps.

They reached a level place in the road, and Federigo sat
down again to rest. He was dizzy from weariness, and every
muscle in his body throbbed; but he was afraid to go to
sleep out in the open—the knights might find him, and
there were supposed to be bandits on this road. Yusuf, of
course, curled right up and went to sleep. Federigo's head
sank down, and his chin rested on his chest. He couldn't
keep his eyes open much longer. . . .

He dozed off. That part of him strong enough to protest
kept nudging his mind, warning him to wake up, and his
sleep was filled with scraps of dreams. Hadji-Mustafa leaning against the tiller, talking about the stars in his strange
soft voice, as if he loved them . . . and Durante as a pirate, leaping with a sword onto a Genoese ship. . . . He
stirred and saw the moon shining on the face of the cliff and
the strange rock just down the road, so square it looked like
a little stone house. Again he slept, and this time dreamed of
a wild charge of ragged bandits, and the screaming of
women, and a baby crying. When he opened his eyes again,
the moon had set.

"Come on, Yusuf, wake up." He pulled Yusuf still half-
sleeping to his feet. "Come on, let's go just a little way."

"Oh, let me sleep, please—" Yusuf's head jerked up. "Do
you hear something?"

Federigo frowned. "No. Just the wind. Come on."

"That isn't the wind."

"It's a bird, then. Come on." He wasn't really sure he
heard the thin wail; it came on and off, like a thing in a
dream. He gave Yusuf a push on down the road, toward the

square rock.

The square rock! He stopped dead and stared. It wasn't a rock, it was a cart, overturned. Yusuf, beside him, gave out a small cry and started forward.

"I told you I heard something." Yusuf broke into a run.

From the shadow of the cart, somebody darted, running from them. Skirts whirled around its legs. Federigo dashed after Yusuf. It was a woman. And the cart . . . the cart had been burned, recently: he could smell charred wood, now that he was closer to it. And the thin cry was the sob of a baby. He tripped over a cartwheel and fell sliding onto the rough earth of the road, got up, and ran on. Yusuf had overtaken the woman and was trying to hold her, talking to her, while she wept and begged him to let her go. Federigo jogged up to them. The woman—she was only a girl—clutched a little baby to her with both arms, and tears covered her face.

"It's all right," Yusuf was saying. "We won't hurt you."

Federigo said, "Hush, girl, there are knights all over the beach just a little way away."

She stopped struggling. "Knights?"

"Somebody's camped down on the beach." He pulled the tail of his shirt out of his trousers and wiped her face. "Don't cry."

"Who are you? I thought you were—" She began to cry again, and Yusuf scooped the baby out of her arms and rocked it, watching her curiously.

"We're friends," Federigo said. He led her back toward the cart, which looked like shelter. "What happened?"

"Oh—oh—" The girl flung her arms around him. "It was terrible."

Federigo pulled her arms free and made her sit down in the eave of the cart. He still had some of the cheese left, and he tore off a chunk of it and gave it to her. "Here. Eat something. What happened?"

"The caravan was attacked," she said, and broke into a wail. Federigo shook his head in exasperation. Holding the baby, Yusuf crooned absently, his eyes on the girl's face.

"Who are you? Where do you live?"

"My name is—is Maria. And I live in the Street of the Jars, in Palermo."

"Palermo!" Yusuf said, softly. "That's where we're going."

"Maria, what happened?" Federigo fed her more cheese. She might be upset, but she ate like any greedy girl.

"Somebody attacked the caravan. I was fetching wood for a fire—I and my baby. When I came back everything was burning, they were all fighting—" She sobbed. "I hid. When I came out, everybody was gone."

"Here?" Federigo looked around. The cartwheel he'd tripped over had come from this cart, and there was no other sign of damage except this one broken vehicle. "They don't seem to have done much."

"They left me here," the girl cried, and burst into tears again.

"She's useless," Yusuf said. "All girls are. What are we going to do with her?"

Federigo shrugged. "She's going to Palermo, and so are we."

"We won't be able to move fast with a woman and a baby."

"We can't just leave her here. She hasn't got the sense to

walk back to Cefalu." He sighed.

The sun was rising; he could see the girl's face more clearly now. Turning, he looked out to sea. The light turned the water gold.

"Let's make up our minds after we've slept," Yusuf said.

Federigo nodded. His weariness had returned, dragging at him, making it hard to think. "All right. Maria, listen to me. Are you listening?"

The girl nodded. She'd taken her baby back from Yusuf, and one hand smoothed the fine dark hair across the baby's skull.

"We're going to sleep—Yusuf and I. My name is—Durante. When we wake up, we'll go to Palermo and take you with us, all right?"

She smiled. "How are two little boys going to get to Palermo?"

"You'll see, when we wake up. If those knights come up here, you must wake us up. Do you understand me?"

"I'm not stupid," she said, loftily.

"I'm glad to hear that." Federigo crawled into the back of the cart, where a heap of old clothes had fallen down to make a kind of bed. "Keep a good watch."

Yusuf crept closer to him. "She's right. How are we going to get to Palermo?"

"Walk." Federigo yawned and put his head down.

"But it's so far."

"There's nothing else to do. Go to sleep."

Yusuf snorted. "You always have all the answers. 'Stow away on a pirate ship.' 'Walk to Palermo.' I don't know why I hang around with you, all you ever do is get me into trouble."

As tired as he was, Federigo had to laugh at that: It was so true. He shut his eyes.

The bright morning sun revealed no new solution to the problem. They divided the last of the cheese among them, and Maria fed the baby. Federigo walked far enough back on the road to see that whoever had camped on the beach the night before was gone, leaving nothing behind except a great blackened ring on the white sand and the marks of many horses. Going back, he found Yusuf arranging a long piece of cloth as a cradle for Maria to carry the baby on her hip.

"They're gone, at least," Federigo said. "Maria, how far is it to Palermo?"

She looked over and shrugged her shoulders carelessly. "Far. It doesn't matter, we'll never get there." She crooned to the baby.

Yusuf said, "She's been talking like that all morning. Why don't we leave her here? She'll only slow us up."

"Because—" Federigo flung his arms out. He could think of no good reason for taking the girl along with them; it was easier to steal food for two than for four, and she wouldn't make the traveling any easier. "I wouldn't like anyone to do that to me," he said. Something in him said, "Do it." He heaved a tremendous sigh. "Let's start walking."

Yusuf made a face. They started out, Maria between them; the road rose up along the side of the cliff, and far below them, the beach glittered stark glaring white in the sun. The boom of the surf reached Federigo's ears only as a faint whispering. He watched his bare feet striding along the road—they were filthy dirty, Franciscus would have been furious. A sense of helplessness overwhelmed him. Each of his strides seemed so short, and it was such a long way to Palermo. Maria was right: They would never get there. He clenched his teeth and walked on.

I'M SO HUNGRY," Maria said and sank down on a hummock of grass by the side of the road. "I'm not going to go any farther until I have something to eat."

Federigo raised his hands and let them fall to his sides. "Where are we going to find food out here?" He looked up at the cliff above them—bare, brown rock, pocked and hollowed and knobbed by the wind.

Yusuf sat down next to Maria. "Don't be silly," he said softly. "We could sit here until we starve. There must be a village close by, maybe just up the road. Come on, keep walking until we get there."

"No." The girl shook her head; her hair came loose from its white scarf, but she ignored it. "I'm hungry." Suddenly she was weeping, great tears rolling down her face. "My husband is dead, my parents are dead, and you want me to walk to Palermo, and my feet hurt." She put her face in her hands.

Federigo wanted to scream. He sank down on his heels

and pulled in empty rage at the tufts of coarse, gray-green grass.

"What are we going to do?" Yusuf said to him.

"I don't know. Maria, maybe your family isn't dead. There was only one cart burned, there was no sign of a real fight. Maybe they scared off the bandits. Maybe they went on."

"Maybe the bandits drove off all the other carts," Maria said.

Federigo shrugged. "Why expect the worst?" He stood up, looking down the road. Perhaps there was a village just around the bend, but he didn't think so. It was a wild sea-coast, and he doubted that anyone lived there at all. It was hard to think of what he should do. Yusuf was staring at his hands, his face grim.

"Go on," the voice in his mind said. "If you don't, no one will." He tried to resist it—he thought of talking Yusuf into going to look for something to eat. But he knew that Yusuf would only go a little way and come back almost at once, saying he'd found nothing. Maria was crying steadily.

"All right," Federigo said. "I'll go look. Yusuf, stay here and keep watch on her."

Yusuf only nodded and stared off to sea. Federigo had an idea of how he felt—he felt lost and frightened, too. Walking fast, he started up the road toward the bend ahead.

"Little Red," Yusuf shouted, and he turned. Yusuf waved his arm. "Be careful."

Federigo waved back and walked on. Sea birds swooped and dove over the rocks ahead of him, and he tried to figure out a way of trapping them. But that would take nets, or a bow and arrow. And he'd need nets to fish. He wondered

how far he should go before he turned back and told them
he'd found nothing. A wild, tense urgency filled him suddenly. He had to find something. He had to. He broke into
a run to the bend in the road.

The road swept around in a long curve and ran on and
on to another jutting headland, and there was no village.
He'd known in his heart there would not be one. Only the
blank sand and the sea and the barren cliff confronted him,
ringing with the cries of the sea birds. He started down the
little slope, scuffing up the dust with his feet.

I wish I were home. I wish I were back in Palermo. The
longing filled him, and he felt that, if he only wished hard
enough, strong enough, he would be magically transported
across the coastline to his own city. The slope turned steep
under his feet, and he leaned back to keep from falling.
Dust fine as flour squirted up between his toes. Just ahead,
a gully cut through the cliff to the road, just a narrow alleyway in the natural wall of rock, full of weeds and brambles.

He yelped. Wheel tracks flattened the heavy grass, and a
pile of cow dung lying in the weeds looked still soft. A cart
had turned down there recently—within the day. He
trotted into the gully, following the tracks. Abruptly, he
stopped, and his heart jumped up into his mouth. Who
would be driving a cart off the road into a lonely, desolate
gully—except bandits?

What Maria had said came back to him. Maybe the
thieves had taken the entire caravan—seized all the people
to sell them into slavery—and driven all the carts up this
gulley into the hills. But immediately he rejected that: The
tracks he was following had been made by only one cart.

Keeping close to the steep rocky side of the gulch, he walked through weeds high as his waist along the track. His ears strained to catch the slightest noise from up ahead; his stomach was fluttery.

Ahead, the gully turned a corner, and he crept around it—and swiftly ducked back into the shelter of the bank. The gully had widened out into a tiny bowl of a valley, full of sweet grass. On it, an ox and a mare grazed, and near the far end was a wagon. A wisp of smoke rose from the fire burning near the wagon's tail gate. It was somebody's camp. He crawled nearer to investigate.

Before the fire there was a woman sitting, kneading bread in a shallow wooden bowl; she had a red scarf wrapped around her head, but tendrils of dark hair escaped from beneath it and she kept brushing them back. A pot, braced up on two rocks, simmered on the fire. Even from that distance, Federigo could smell meat and broth, and his stomach cramped up with hunger. He lay down in the high grass to watch and wait.

After a few moments, a tall man walked into the little camp, carrying two dead hares by their hind legs. He spoke to the woman, who nodded, and went off a little way to skin out the carcasses. A boy a little older than Federigo followed him, swinging a bow and two bloody arrows. Federigo murmured under his breath. He thought the man had spoken Italian to the woman, but he wasn't sure—it sounded like a dialect. He'd never seen people like that before. Like all Sicilian wagons, theirs was painted in bright red, yellow, green and blue, but he recognized none of the patterns; they didn't seem to make a story.

The woman set out the bread to rise and began to make a

kind of oven out of rocks—piling them carefully into a
dome, with a place on the bottom for the bread and an open
ring on top for hot coals. A colt appeared in the meadow,
bumped its head impatiently against the flank of the mare,
and drank. Obviously, the lower part of the meadow,
which Federigo could not see, was fairly large, and probably there was water there, a spring, or maybe a brook. He
was thirsty at the thought of it.

Laughing and making jokes he couldn't hear, the man
and the boy hung the skinned hares off the tail gate of the
wagon and went off down the meadow. Federigo crawled a
little closer. If he could steal one of the hares, they'd find a
way to cook it, back on the road. And meat would be good
after all the cheese and bread they'd been eating. He waited
in the grass for the woman to go out of sight.

She looked over her bread, poked up the fire, and sat
down to mend a shirt. Federigo hissed under his breath.
Flashing in the sun, her needle dove in and out of the white
cloth, and he put his head down, itching all over with impatience. Finally she was done, she shook out the shirt and
inspected it, put it in the wagon, and took out a whole load
of clothes. Federigo almost groaned with frustration. But
these clothes, apparently, she meant to wash; she took a pail
and started in the same direction the men had taken, singing
softly as she walked. Federigo got up and dashed to the
wagon. The hares hung by their naked heels from the tail
gate, and he snatched one and lifted it off the hook.

A horrible growl sounded right in his ears and turned
him cold as ice. Whirling, he faced an enormous black dog
that had been lying, all along, under the wagon. The dog
was on its feet, its head lowered, and its white teeth showed

in an ugly fringe beneath its curled lips.

Federigo yelped, bounded to the fire, and grabbed a burning stick from it. The dog caught his shirt in its teeth. With a tremendous wrench, it nearly pulled the boy off his feet; he swung the branch with all his strength at the dog's head, and embers rained down on both of them.

"Aci, hold!" the man roared, in his odd Italian. Glancing over his shoulder, Federigo saw him racing up toward him, the boy behind him, and he smacked the dog with his fists, trying to run away. The dog growled and braced itself, hanging onto his shirt; the shirt tore, and Federigo twisted loose entirely and took three running strides toward the road.

The fourth stride was as long and hard as the others, but he was no longer on the ground. The man had picked him up by the arms. Federigo kicked, shouted, flung himself around, and tried to bite the hands holding him. They'll murder me, he thought. They'll take me to Diepold. He struck out awkwardly with his fists, but the man was behind him.

"Little tiger," the man grumbled. "Boy! Boy, be still, or I'll turn the dog on you."

"Let me go," Federigo shouted. "Let me go or I'll—"

Something hit him so hard on the side of the head that his eyes lost their sight and his ears roared. The ground struck him on the side. He lay still, panting, trying to keep from losing consciousness. Gradually, the world stopped swinging around him, the ground stopped tilting under him, and he sat up, his hands to his face.

"Thief," the man said. "Do you know what happens to thieves, boy? Do you?"

Federigo wiped his face on his torn shirt and said nothing. The smear of dirt and sweat on the ripped cloth embarrassed him a little; they'd think he was dirty all the time. Well, he was, actually. He thought of Yusuf and Maria; somehow, he had to talk his way out of this.

"He was trying to make off with the hare," the boy said. He hung up the carcass on the tail gate again and spoke to the dog, which wagged its tail and licked the boy's hand.

"What did you want a hare for?" the man said. He nudged Federigo with his foot. "Talk."

"I was hungry," Federigo said.

"How could you be hungry? The coast is full of food."

The woman said quietly, "Maybe he doesn't know how to get it, Simone. He's a city boy—look at him."

Simone scratched his cheek, eying Federigo. "Who are you?"

"My name is Durante. I live in Palermo."

"In Palermo? What are you doing here?"

"I . . . went to Cefalu for a while. Please, let me go, I won't bother you anymore. Not with the dog there."

The woman took a wooden bowl from the wagon and ladled stew from the pot on the fire into it.

Angrily, the boy said, "Mama, you aren't going to—"

"Be quiet," Simone said. "He's small, he's far from home, and he's hungry."

Federigo gulped. They were going to feed him, even though they'd caught him trying to steal from them. Suddenly he felt miserable and wicked. He put his hands up to his face.

"There's no sense being penitent now," Simone said. "Here, eat some of this."

Federigo looked up. The woman was holding out the bowl; she smiled encouragingly and nodded to him. He took the bowl and sniffed the blended aromas of herbs, broth and goat meat, tiny wild vegetables, and the bit of bread she'd put in the bowl along with the stew. He swallowed the saliva that filled his mouth.

"No," he said. "I tried to steal it, you shouldn't give it to me."

The boy made a sound in his throat. Squatting, Simone cocked his head to one side and stared at Federigo.

The woman said, "Don't be silly. You're hungry. Eat. We have more than we need."

Simone said mildly, "If it will make you feel better, city boy, I stole the goat."

Startled, Federigo had to laugh, and smiles appeared on the faces of the three people watching him. He ate quickly, although it was so hot he burned his lips and tongue, but the bread he saved to take back to Maria. Immediately he felt guilty about not saving some of the stew for them, and he wondered about asking these people if he could bring his friends here.

But Simone was wrapping the hare in a large leaf. When Federigo put the bowl down, the woman took it and quietly put it in a pail to be washed, and Simone held out the hare.

"If you had asked, I would have given it to you. There are thousands of hares here, you should learn to trap." He shook his head; he looked angry again. "You shouldn't steal, boy."

Federigo stood up, the hare in his hand, and the dog growled again.

Simone said sharply, "Aci, be quiet." Turning to Federigo again, he said, "Go back to Palermo. You'll never survive out here. There are very few people to steal from."

"Who did you steal the goat from, Master?" Federigo
said.

Simone grinned. "God."

Federigo stood watching him a moment, a little awed. He
wished he knew how to live off the land, like these people.
They looked so content. Finally, he bowed. "Thank you."

They said nothing, only watched him, and he trotted
back across the meadow toward the mouth of the gully.
When he reached it, he turned and waved, and to his surprise the boy waved back. Simone was already going on
down to the lower end of the meadow again. He thought of
how free they were. They could go anywhere, they had no
need to stay in one place. The memory of Hadji-Mustafa,
leaning against the stern of his ship watching the stars, came
into his mind. He jogged down the gully to the road, carrying the hare.

"He can steal anything," Yusuf said to Maria and tore
flesh from the roast hare with his fingers, wincing at the
heat.

"I told you, I didn't steal it. I met some people who gave
it to me."

Yusuf frowned at him; clearly, he didn't believe that.
"Well, it doesn't matter. We're eating. How far is it to the
village?"

"There is no village," Federigo cried. "I told you."

Maria licked grease from her chin and rocked the baby
gently in her arms. "Now what do we do?"

"Walk some more." It was already late in the afternoon, and the heat of the day was subsiding. "It'll be cooler, at least." He sucked on a bare bone. The hare had been delicious, what little he'd eaten of it. Yusuf and Maria had devoured almost all of it. But of course Federigo had eaten with the wanderers. He poked at the fire, which Yusuf had made; Yusuf was revealing surprising abilities. Federigo had had no idea of how to build and start a fire.

"Can't we rest a little before—"

"You rested all day," Federigo said. "If we rest all the time, we won't get anywhere. Come on." He stood up. After eating so much, he was drowsy, but he tried to act lively and energetic, an example for them. It was hard. All he wanted was to lie in the sun and doze. With Yusuf, he kicked apart the fire, while Maria sighed and fussed and settled the baby in its sling on her hip. The baby was gurgling and waving its fists around.

"Is that a girl or a boy?" Federigo said, looking at it.

"A boy. His name is Raffaello." She stroked the baby's cap of dark hair.

"That's nice." Federigo started down the road, swinging his arms. Calling to him to wait, the others pulled themselves together and rushed after him, but he didn't wait; it was still a long way to Palermo. Thinking about that lost him some of his confidence. He lengthened his stride.

They walked until well after midnight. The road had risen all the way to the top of the cliff. At the top Federigo was sure that they were near a village—several times, he thought he smelled smoke, and up ahead of them, on the coastline, lights gleamed on and off, like fallen stars among the rocks. They found a wide field and went to sleep under

a tree in the middle of it, all curled up together because the
night was chilly and they had no way to get out of the
constant, cold wind.

The first crack of thunder brought Federigo leaping out
of a sound sleep, with every hair on his head standing on
end. It was still dark, but the wind had risen to a roar. For a
frozen moment, he stared into the sky above the branches
of the tree, tossing wildly like sea waves; lightning flashed
and flashed and flashed again, so that the sky was never
darker than a pale, evil silver, and the thunder split his ears.
The stink of lightning close by reached his nostrils.

He was soaking wet; gradually, he realized that rain was
drenching him, pouring down over him from the wild sky
and streaming along the ground and through his clothes.
He drew a deep breath, still startled. His arms were trembling. Suddenly, through the tremendous bellowing of the
thunder, he heard a strange whimper, and the howl of the
baby.

"Maria," he shouted. "Don't let the baby get wet."

"I've got him, Little Red," Yusuf said, in a frightened
voice. "What's happening?"

"It's a thunderstorm, idiot." The last two words were
drowned in a clap of thunder that stopped up his ears.
Lightning forked through the sky, tearing across the wild,
heaving clouds. The constant flicker of light made the
trees look grotesque, like inhuman hands printed against the
sky. Federigo got up and stumbled toward Yusuf and
Maria. The soggy ground squished under his feet.

A flash of brilliant light filled his eyes and seemed to pen-
etrate into his head; at the same time, like two huge boul-
ders smashing together, thunder rolled, hurtful to hear. He

held his breath, terrified. It had hit somewhere close, very close. He thought wildly that the ground might heave open and swallow him, but gradually he was able to see again —the trees thrashing helplessly under the savage wind. He knelt beside the girl huddled on the ground.

"Maria. Maria." He grabbed her shoulders and shook her. She was praying in a broken voice, her hands clawing her face, and her hair hung in strands all over her cheeks and in her eyes. Yusuf was bending over the baby to keep the rain off it, and it was screeching at the top of its lungs.

"Little Red, we have to get out of the trees."

"I know. Run. I'll bring her."

"God is punishing us," Maria sobbed. "Holy Mary, save me. Saint Peter—"

Yusuf got up and ran, carrying the baby tenderly in his arms. Federigo swiped his sodden hair out of his eyes. "Maria, come on, God isn't punishing anybody. Why would God send a storm like this just to punish us?" He pulled her onto her feet and dragged her out toward the open. Yusuf was already halfway to the road.

Lightning flashed right above them, and the thunder nearly knocked them down.

Maria screamed. "Oh, Jesus in Heaven—"

"Shut up," Federigo roared. "Come on." He hauled her off into the mud and streaming water of the open meadow. The sky was bright, bright white, constantly white, from the incessant lightning. Federigo fell into a hole and landed on his face in the mud. Scrambling up, he looked for Maria.

She was kneeling, babbling prayers, while all around the storm crashed and raged. Out of the shelter of the trees,

they were exposed to the full, slamming violence of the rain, and Federigo had trouble getting up. He took Maria's hand.

"Run!"

Her eyes shut tight, she ran, calling the names of saints. Straight ahead of them stood a strange, forked tree—he couldn't remember seeing it before. Blue fire ran up and down the fork, and he understood: The lightning had struck it. Frightened himself, he ran slipping and sliding over the mud, dragging Maria behind him, to the side of the road.

Yusuf was crouching over the baby, his back to the wind. Federigo sank down beside him. The rain poured down the road in a river, in a tide, and just beyond it, at the edge of the cliff, he could see the white foam of spray. The waves were breaking so hard they reached all the way to the top of the cliff. He gasped.

Maria was panting, silent for once, and with Yusuf she bent over the baby to protect it. Tiny and weak, the infant's shrieks barely reached Federigo's ears over the gigantic cacophony of the storm.

Getting to his feet, he walked toward the cliff's edge, pushing against the wind that shoved and buffeted him. From the rim of the cliff, he could see the waves surging against the rocks so far below, boiling, pounding. It was beautiful. As far as he could see, the wild water tossed and heaved up into giant waves, crested and ridged with foam. The lightning ran in jagged fingers down the sky; beneath it, the sea ran glittering and smoking. He took a deep breath —the wildness of it delighted him, the uncontrollable action. Sitting down, he watched the sea and the storm all the rest of the night, until, with the dawn, the last flicker of

lightning and the last mutter of thunder faded and were
gone.

"He doesn't seem to be sick at all," Yusuf said. He patted
the baby's forehead. "I don't think he got very wet—he
was scared, mostly."

Federigo shrugged. "Good. Then we can get going."

Maria said, "But I'm so tired, I didn't get any sleep at all
last night."

Yusuf made a face. "There's a village up ahead, isn't
there, Little Red? Come on, Maria, we'll go to the village
and maybe someone will give us a place to spend the night.
Let's go, up on your feet."

"My feet hurt," Maria said. She stuck out her bare feet,
covered with dust. "Look how dirty I am."

Federigo danced with rage. Kneeling, Yusuf scrubbed
Maria's feet with his hands. "We can bathe in the village.
Now, come on, Maria, we have to go sometime, why not
now?"

Maria sniffed and turned her eyes on Federigo. "I like
you better than him," she said to Yusuf. "You're nice to
me." She pulled her feet under her and stood up.

"I really don't care whether you like me," Federigo said,
"as long as you start walking." He glared at her, and she
glared back. They started down the road, Maria leaning on
Yusuf's shoulder, while Yusuf carried the baby.

After the storm, the air tasted cleaner and sweeter, and
the sky almost glowed, it was so blue. Federigo was hungry
again, but now he was used to not eating. He glanced out to
sea—he'd seen a ship that morning, and he was wondering if
it were Hadji-Mustafa's. Durante would be learning to

make sail, to steer and pull an oar and navigate. Durante's feet wouldn't burn and his stomach growl; Durante was safe and warm at night. Except that Federigo didn't like the idea of being on the sea during a storm. The waves had looked as if they could have broken up a ship in moments, torn it to bits and flung the wreckage on the shore. There's good and bad in everything, as it says in books, he thought.

The road slanted down under his feet. He found a long stick lying beside the road and picked it up to use as a walking staff. Walking was boring—he was sick of it. When I am grown up and really King, he thought, I'll never walk anywhere; I'll always ride.

That reminded him of Diepold. They had to be careful in the village; they had to watch for knights, for people staring at him as if they recognized him. He twitched all over. Good and bad in everything. If you weren't starving, you were hiding and running. He glanced at Maria, who was still leaning on Yusuf.

They walked down a steep slope and around a bend in the road, and there ahead of them lay the village, only a little way off.

Yusuf gave a glad shout. "Little Red, look."

"I see." Federigo walked over to him. Putting his mouth close to Yusuf's ear, he whispered, "Maybe you'd better go in without me, and I'll meet you on the other side. Can you beg some food?"

Yusuf frowned, puzzled. "But why—oh." He glanced at Maria. "Of course. Well, I can try, anyhow. There might be Saracens there, I'll beg alms from them. Where shall we meet you?"

"I'll be on the road just the other—wait." He stepped

back, looking behind them; a cart was making its way down the slope, piled high with bolts of cloth and bales of wool. The drover walked along beside his ox, guiding it with a long stick. Federigo shaded his eyes to study the man, while Yusuf and Maria sat down in the grass at the edge of the road.

"Good morning, Master," Federigo said, when the cart was drawing up abreast of them.

"Good morning," the drover said, eying them suspiciously. He called to his ox and yanked on the line that ran to the ring in the beast's nose, and the ox stopped.

"Can you tell us the name of this village?" Federigo asked, as politely as he could sound.

"That's San Sebastiano." The drover eyed Yusuf and Maria. "Where are you bound?"

"There, for now. At least, my friends are. For the mercy of Jesus, could you take them with you? We don't know this region very well."

The drover pulled at his lower lip. His small dark eyes flickered from Federigo to the two sitting by the road. After a moment, he said, "The girl can ride in the cart, if she wants. No sense in making a mother and her child walk. The boy can follow. Where are you going, redhead?"

"There," Federigo said, waving vaguely toward the hills behind them. "Thank you, Master. God have mercy on you for having mercy on them." Turning, he ran off into the field behind the road, as if he actually were going someplace. When he'd gone a little distance, he wheeled and watched.

The drover and Yusuf were helping Maria into the cart; she settled herself comfortably on the pile of wool and cloth. Talking energetically, Yusuf helped the drover get the ox moving again and walked along beside him, nodding and gesturing with both hands. Federigo grinned. Yusuf would talk the drover into getting them something to eat and maybe even a place to stay. If not, they could always hang around the square.

He started off at a dogtrot toward the village, swerving so that he could sneak in through the back streets. He knew the name San Sebastiano—there was a village by that name only a day's journey from Palermo. While he ran, he glanced critically at the sun. The bulk of the day lay still before him. He would wait until dark to go into the village; and when he did, he had some things to find out. After he'd crossed the field, when he was near enough to San Sebastiano to smell the stench of all villages—garbage, cooking fires, the harbor—he curled up under a tree, shaded his eyes from the sun with his arms, and fell asleep. Tonight, he had many things to do.

Trotting through alleys, leaping mounds of trash, sneaking around corners, Federigo made his way toward the square. It was full dark. Most of the houses he'd passed were shuttered and locked, and he'd heard someone snoring when he walked under a window. At the edge of the square, he stopped and leaned against the stone wall of the next building; the wall was still warm from the day's heat.

In the center of the square, a fountain bubbled and spouted water in gentle arcs into the air. The refuse of a market day covered the cobblestones—orange peels, leaves from vegetables already limp and brown, and patches of hay. Under a palm tree near the fountain, a loose goat was eating whatever it could find; a rope trailed from its neck, chewed through or broken. There was no sign of people.

Directly across the way stood a large stone church. Federigo ran through the middle of the square and up the short flight of steps to the door, which stood ajar. Easing his way through it, he looked quickly all around. Candles burned before the altar; a huge crucifix hung above them, half-buried in shadow. Two old women were kneeling near the front of the church, but one was snoring. Whatever vigil they kept, it was less important than their sleep. He backed out onto the porch again and walked its length, jumped down to the ground, and loped around behind the church.

As he'd suspected, there was a stable there. He'd seen no building in the town fine enough to house knights; but wherever they slept, they'd keep their horses here. He groped around the long, low stable wall until he found a window, and stood on his toes to look in.

All the stalls were empty except one, which held a light palfrey, no knight's horse. On a pile of straw near the front door two people lay sleeping. Yusuf and Maria. Federigo snorted. If he'd stayed outside the town waiting for them, he'd have waited all night and well into the day. Yusuf was lazy, too. Letting himself down from the window, Federigo looked around for another way to find out if there were knights in the town.

On another side of the square was a stone building that looked very official; a porch ran its whole front length, covered with climbing vines and flowers. He started toward it, but before he'd gone halfway across the square toward it, he heard soft giggles and the murmur of voices behind the veil of flowers. There were boys and girls in there, courting. Federigo drifted off into the darkness. It was time to find something to eat.

He walked down a side street, following the information of his nose: Someone up that way had baked bread recently. It was darker there than in the square, the buildings shut off the light from the sky, and the eaves of the roofs overhung the street. He caught the dull gleam of an open window ahead, and walked faster.

"Federigo."

The hair on the back of his neck prickled up, he stopped dead. In the dark alleyway just behind him, there was a laugh as soft and cracked as the rattle of dry leaves over pebbles.

"Federigo."

"Who's there?" He peered into the darkness, but he saw no one.

"Come and find out, Federigo."

His heart was hammering in his side, and he dried his sweating palms on his shirt. I might go in there and . . . He thought of knives in the dark, of demons in the gloom of the alleyway. I know there are no ghosts. But his feet wanted to run down the cobbled street to the safety of the square, to the chatter of the voices behind the veil of flowers. Slowly, unwillingly, he crept into the alleyway.

"I won't hurt you," the old, dry voice crooned. "Come and find me, Federigo."

A fat furry body scurried away through heaps of rubbish, and something clattered in the dark. He smelled garlic and rotting garbage. Suddenly, a few steps in front of him, a tiny blue light glowed and grew stronger and revealed the seamed, wizened face of a witch.

Federigo stopped dead. He'd seen a witch only once before—one of the old, old women from the hills who knew which herbs made you better and which made you die, and who cast spells, lifted spells, and told the future. He wasn't sure he believed in them, but he was very sure he was afraid of them. She grinned at him—she had only one tooth in her lower jaw, like a fang, and her gray hair stuck out in all directions. She stretched out one hand.

"Come, come. Who could harm the King of Sicily? Are you not an Emperor's son? Sit down, and I will tell you what you have to know before you reach Palermo."

Trembling all over, he sank down on his heels. The old woman put down her lamp between them. She wore black rags, and around her neck hung strings and strings of amulets sewn into little leather pouches. While he stared, amazed, she reached across the lamp and took his hands.

"Are you afraid of witches, Federigo?"

"No."

"Do you believe in witches, Federigo?"

"No," he whispered.

She laughed. "When you were born," she said, in her whispering voice, "a monk in the north had a vision during the night. He was a Christian, but still he had a vision of the future. And he said that you would destroy everything that stood against you. But he didn't know then that your father and mother would die and leave you alone."

Federigo said evenly, "Whenever princes are born, people say strange things."

"But not what they said of you, Federigo. Before you were born they said that you were the long-awaited child who would bring forth and rule over the new world."

All along Federigo's back, the skin grew cold with an ominous prickling. In the blue light the face of the witch seemed to change shapes, one moment young and smooth, and the next even older than when he'd seen her first, like a skull. He shuddered. In her grip his hands tensed. But she was much stronger than he'd imagined, she held him fast.

"The lamb torn but not destroyed, the lion among his own, and still, you are a little boy, a ragged little boy with long red hair, running off on adventures. The girl with you, Federigo, and her baby, you must take them home. All the way home, to the Street of the Jars, in Palermo."

"How did you know where—"

"I know what it is given to me to know. I know what I must know." She laughed so softly he could hardly hear it. "The girl is in your keeping, and you must carry it through, or all your life you will carry nothing through to its end."

That made sense. He nodded, his eyes intent on her face.

"You will live a strange and terrible life, Federigo. You shall sail over the sea, and journey into the dark forests of the north, you shall reign over many peoples. You shall have many women, and many men will seek your favor, even kings. But you shall trust few, and love fewer still, and fewest of all shall be those who will love you. You will never be alone, and yet all your life you will be lonely."

"Tell me," he said, "that I will be a great king, and that won't matter."

"It will matter," she said. "It will matter. You will walk through the world in such splendor that all those around you will be struck with awe and amazement, but none shall understand you. You will have many enemies, none of them worthy of you. Every time you strike against one, you will defeat him, but a dozen more will attack you from behind. All your life you will be victorious, but when you die they will sweep aside your victories and all you have won and try to destroy it, and not for many, many years will the world understand what you have done. Are you frightened?"

"No. No."

"You shall be more than a great king, Federigo. You shall be a great Emperor; and while you are still in the prime of your life, men will speak of you as The Wonder of the World."

He laughed, overjoyed. "I don't care, then—I don't care what else happens."

"You will." The voice of the witch seemed to fade, to go out like a candle, and her lamp dimmed. "You will care, much, much later." Her hand passed over the lamp, and the blue light flashed and vanished. Federigo cried out in surprise and stood up. Stumbling in the darkness, he searched for her, but she was gone, and the lamp was gone, and all that he found was a heap of dusty rags and a cat that yowled at him, leaped up onto a rooftop, and disappeared into the night.

"Yusuf?"

"Unnnnh?"

"Wake up—we have to go." Federigo thought of telling him about the witch, but just thinking about it kept him quiet. He wasn't really sure it had happened, somehow. He wasn't sure how to think about it. He pushed Yusuf until he got to his feet, stretching and yawning. Maria rolled over, comfortable in the straw.

"We're only a day's walk from Palermo," Yusuf said. "Only a day away."

"Are we starting off again?" Maria said, whining. She picked up the baby. "Let me sleep a little more."

Yusuf snorted. "I'm so sick of her complaining, Little Red—she can get home by herself from here, can't she?"

"No. Come on, Maria, get up."

"You're horrible. You're the most wretched little beast of a boy—" Maria grunted and stood up, hugging the baby. "You're wearing me to the bone. Look, it isn't even light out yet."

"Have you eaten?" Yusuf said. "We have some bread and a little cheese."

"Somebody left pies out to cool. I ate for half the night." He thought, I'll never steal anything else, I promise. Unless I have to, of course. He shrugged. "Did you see any knights?"

"No, but the drover says they've been riding up and down the highroad for days. They are saying that you're dead. They're saying Diepold murdered you."

"Ssssh." Federigo glanced at Maria. "Come on."

They went out of the stable into the clear, rosy light of the first dawn and walked through the square toward the road to Palermo. Yusuf stretched his arms over his head.

"I can't wait to get home. Wait until I tell my father where I've been. What are you going to tell Diepold?"

Federigo sighed. "Nothing. I'll just take my shirt off and bend over and let him whip me until his arm falls off. Did you hear anything about Walter of Brienne?"

"No, but the Papal Legate has gone to Rome again."

"Good. I'm safe, then."

They passed the last houses of the village and walked down the road with plowed fields on one side and the sea on the other. Fishing boats rocked on the water just beyond the surf, with men scrambling around their sterns rigging nets. Yusuf took out his bread and ate some of it, breaking off bits of the soft inside for Maria. In the sling on her hip, the baby slept soundly, his fist pressed against his cheek.

Yusuf began to sing a Saracen song; he drew out the end of each note into a flourish and beat time with his hands.

Federigo thought, the man in the pleasure house who wanted me dead said I should never have been born. The witch said I was born to rule over a new world. Which one is right? He wanted to believe the witch—he wanted desperately to grow up into the man she had spoken of, walking in splendor, the awe of the world. If he wanted it hard enough, maybe it would come true. If he wanted it hard enough that he'd do anything to get it, maybe it would come true. A strange and terrible life, she had said. He shuddered.

"Yusuf, do you believe in witchcraft?"

"Of course. Witches know things other people can't know."

Maybe.

At noon, they came up to a fork in the road, marked by a tall stone cross. Around its foot stood three horses. Federigo hung back, shy, and wished he had a hood to cover his red hair. The man and woman who sat in the saddles of two of the horses were noble—he could tell by their fine clothes and the sleekness of their horses. A second man was fixing the girth of the lady's horse. Federigo stayed behind Maria, keeping his head down.

"Good day, my lords," Yusuf said, bowing. He stuck his hand out. "In the name of God—"

The man on the horse took a coin from his purse and threw it to him. While Yusuf picked up the coin from the dust, the mounted man turned to the lady and said, "There are beggars everywhere, these days."

The lady had been staring at Federigo, trying to make him out behind the bulk of Maria's skirts. Bending toward her lord, she murmured something, and Federigo tensed to run. But the lord only snorted.

"He's dead," the lord said casually, looking off. "This great search for him is only Diepold's foolish way of staving off the inevitable. Marino, aren't you done yet?"

"Now, my lord." Marino stepped back, pulled the skirts of the lady's saddle straight, and went to his own horse, which stood, reins trailing, directly beneath the stone cross. He mounted, and the three trotted away along the road to Palermo. Federigo sighed in relief.

"Who are you?" Maria muttered, looking down at him. "Who are you that you can't walk openly into villages and you hide from lords and ladies?"

Federigo drifted away from her. "What did they give you, Yusuf? A taren?"

"No," Maria called. "Wait." She tossed her head to throw her hair out of her eyes; her face was flushed and her eyes shone. "The King is dead, they all say so, and that's what those people were talking about—"

"Be quiet," Yusuf said. "Whatever you think, think it, but keep quiet." He held out a small copper coin to Federigo.

Maria put her hand out and touched Federigo's hair. "Where did you get such hair?"

"My father was a German." They walked on, but Maria kept close to him, which made him uneasy.

"So was the father of the King a German."

"I can't help that." He knocked aside her hand. "Leave me alone."

Maria hung back, whispering to Yusuf, who shrugged, looked away, and finally shouted, "Leave me alone—he's just a boy of Palermo, that's all, and he's afraid of knights." He ran to catch up to Federigo.

"She knows," Federigo said. "It makes no difference. We'll be home by nightfall." At the thought, he felt queasy; he wasn't entirely sure he'd be safe back there. Maybe they'd still try to . . . Diepold now might want him gone, too. Buried in his thoughts, he strode blindly down the road.

The rumble of hoofbeats behind him jarred him into sudden watchfulness. Whirling, he saw the dust cloud coming down the road after them, and without even thinking about it he jumped into the ditch along the seaward edge. Maria cried out, but Yusuf grabbed her by the arm and pulled her over to the side of the road. Federigo heard him whisper, "Say nothing. Do nothing. Stand still." In the ditch, Federigo hid himself under a drifted mass of branches and leaves. His blood thundered in his ears, blotting out the pound of hoofs, but he could feel the ground tremble under him.

The horsemen raced down on them and reined up, and a voice Federigo knew called, "You. Boy. Come here."

That was Lothair. Federigo held his breath. If they found him—if they found him—he wondered what would happen. He wouldn't be able to take Maria all the way home, and the witch had said—

"Yes, Master?" Yusuf was saying.

"How long have you traveled this road?"

"From the—from the crossroads back there," Yusuf said. To Federigo, his voice sounded as if he were lying, tight

and too high, but Lothair might not hear that. He pressed himself against the side of the ditch.

"Have you seen a boy about your age, a little shorter than you, with red hair? With pale eyes?"

"No," Yusuf said. "I've seen no one except a—a lord and a lady and their servant. They went that way."

One of the men with Lothair said, "Who would that be?"

"It doesn't matter," Lothair said. "Boy, are you sure? Did you pass through a village called San Sebastiano?"

"No," Yusuf said, and Federigo silently applauded him for keeping his head. "I came down that crossroad, I've seen no village."

Lothair swore; abruptly the hoofs drummed on the ground, a terrific beating, and charged off along the road.

Maria said, "He is the King. He is the King, and I never knew."

"Federigo," Yusuf said, "you can come out now, they're gone."

Federigo climbed up the side of the ditch. "Good. You did the right thing." He hugged Yusuf. "They must have heard about me in San Sebastiano. Someone must have seen me."

Maria fell to her knees and grabbed Federigo by the shirt. "My lord, my lord."

"Oh, be quiet. You hated me when you didn't know who I was. Come on. We have to be careful now." He thought, Lothair knows I'm alive. When he catches up to the nobles, they'll tell him there was a redheaded boy with Yusuf and Maria. He broke into a run, too excited to keep still, and realized that he couldn't run all the way to Palermo. On the inland side of the road, the cliffs rose in a steep rise of rock.

He looked up at them.

"We have to go up there."

"What?" Yusuf turned to look up. "Why?"

"They'll come back looking for all of us. Let's go."

He jogged along the cliff's foot, looking for a way to climb up. For a moment, looking hopelessly at the unbroken stone, he thought, let them find me. They'll only take me where I want to go anyway. But they'd come this far alone. And the witch had said he had to take Maria home. He found a place where the rock was cleft in a long fissure and started to climb.

"Hang onto me, Maria. It won't be as hard as it looks."

He felt her hand take hold of his shirttail. Ripped as it was, old and worn, it wouldn't hold if she fell. But he needed both hands to help him climb. He scrambled up to the end of the fissure and reached behind him.

"Here, hold my hand." Ahead, a narrow ledge ran a little way farther up. He crept out on it, clinging with one hand to the knobs and hollows in the rock. The ledge was barely wide enough to put both feet on at once. Glancing down, he saw the road already far below them, and he thought of falling and shut his eyes a moment. "Don't look down." Edging his way along the ledge, he searched for a way up.

"Little Red, there's a chimney—" Yusuf caught his breath, and Federigo heard pebbles bounce down the side of the cliff in a tiny avalanche. He looked up over his head. There, the rock had split into a narrow gap that widened as it reached the top—a chimney, as Yusuf had called it. He let go of Maria's hand and she whimpered.

"Ssssh."

The chimney began well above his head. When he

reached up, he could just touch the bottom of the crack. He pressed himself against the face of the cliff and groped with his toes for a foothold. The ball of his foot found a tiny flattened place on the cliff, and he pushed himself carefully up, reached into the chimney, and found a knob of rock to hang onto. Pulling with his hand and pushing with both feet, he scrambled up into the bottom of the chimney. The harsh rock scraped his knees and elbows, and his blood dribbled across the stone, following a minute scratch like a tiny river. He wedged himself into the chimney and reached down for Maria's hand.

"I can't," she sobbed. Tears slobbered her face. "I can't —I can't—"

Yusuf was holding the baby. "Go up a little, Federigo— give her room."

With his feet against one side of the crack, his back against the other, Federigo slid up a little way. "Now I can't reach her."

"Maria," Yusuf said, "here." He braced himself on the narrow ledge, cradling the baby awkwardly, and slapped his thigh. "Stand on me."

"You'll fall," she said. "And my baby—"

The baby let out a howl. Federigo shut his eyes. This was almost funny. It was the kind of thing that would be uproariously funny once it was over, but while it happened he wanted to explode with frustration. He leaned down, trying not to see the road so far below, and grabbed Maria's wrist.

"Push! Come on, girl, climb."

She began to pray again; clawing at the rock with her free hand, shoving her feet against the stone, she dragged herself up into the chimney and landed square in Federigo's lap. Her skirts covered his face, and she managed to kick him in the knee. He grabbed her and pushed her away from him, deeper into the chimney.

"Get away from me, you—Maria, can't you do anything? No, I'll get the baby. There, see all the footholds and handholds?" He put his hands on her rump and shoved, and with a squeal Maria started to climb wildly toward the top of the cliff. Inside the chimney there were small ledges, little bushes, knobs and protrusions—she found them all in one mad scramble along the face of the rock, like a spider going up a wall. Federigo shook his head.

"Give me the baby."

Yusuf held the baby up toward him—it was wiggling and screaming as if it wanted to throw itself off the cliff, and Federigo laid it on the rock beside him, with his body between it and the long drop. The baby's roars re-echoed against the rock.

"My baby," Maria howled, up on the top of the cliff.

"Shut up," Federigo shouted. "Yusuf, here." He reached down for him. Yusuf glanced up, caught his wrist, and pulled himself easily up into the chimney. He paused just long enough to grin at Federigo, snatched up the baby, and climbed swiftly up to Maria. An instant after he'd reached her, both her screams and those of the baby cut off in the middle.

"He threw her off," Federigo muttered. Aching all over from the scrapes and bruises and being stepped on, he made his way to the top and lay down flat in soft, sweet grass.

Maria was feeding the baby, her face smooth and un-clouded. Yusuf said softly, "We should have given her to the knights to take home. One of them was that big German who chases you around all the time."

"I know." Federigo got up. "Well, we'd better get moving."

From the top of the cliff, the view was much different. He could see more of the sea and much, much more of the land—enough of the land to see that Lothair and the knights were still galloping up the road away from them, far, far down the coast. They dragged Maria to her feet and started off.

"Here they come," Yusuf said. "I'm hungry again."

"So am I. I can't remember ever not being hungry." Federigo shaded his eyes and saw the dust cloud boiling back down the road. "They must have met the nobles."

Yusuf nodded. They walked back away from the edge of the cliff. After they could no longer see the knights coming, Federigo got an unbearable urge to go back and yell insults and taunts at them, to show them that he'd gotten away from them again. He kept craning his neck to see. The cliff cut off all the sound; he had no idea how close they were. Finally he told Yusuf and Maria to keep on going and crept back to the edge of the cliff.

The knights were almost directly beneath him. He watched them slow—he watched Lothair stand in his stirrups and look down the road. Lothair had seen that they weren't around, that they were no longer where he had seen them last. The knights milled around. Seen from above, they looked odd—the horses broad at the hips and narrow at the shoulders, and the men apparently no taller than children. Lothair turned and gave orders, and two of the four knights rode off down the road toward San Sebastiano. Federigo thought they were going to check the crossroads. He lay down on the edge of the cliff and laid his chin on his folded arms, grinning.

Abruptly, Lothair looked straight up at him. Federigo turned cold. But Lothair didn't see him; he looked out toward the sea, shook his head, and thought. One of the remaining two knights dismounted and ran his hands over his horse's forelegs.

Swinging his arm, Lothair spurred his horse into a gallop along the foot of the cliff. Federigo pushed himself up on his knees, frowning, trying to see what they were doing. They disappeared around a bend in the road, but a moment later were visible again when the coast curved out to sea, back where Federigo had climbed the cliff. Lothair slowed his horse to a canter; he was looking up at the cliff. Federigo's opinion of his intelligence began to rise.

Jerking his horse to a stop, Lothair leaned out from the saddle and touched the cliff. Apparently he picked something off the rock; he settled back into his saddle, looked at his fingers, and showed them to another knight, who nodded. Lothair stared up at the top of the cliff. Turning his horse, he started back toward Federigo at a lope, his eyes on the cliff.

Federigo murmured under his breath. Leaping up, he ran back toward Yusuf and Maria, who were already far down the cliff. The sky was clouding over, and a chilly wind blasted him, fluttering his shirt out from his body. When he reached them, he was too short of breath to talk, and he walked along beside them, panting, while Yusuf watched him and waited for him to speak.

"He knows—" Federigo gulped air. "He knows we're here. I don't know—whether he can get up here. We have to hurry."

"We're not that far," Yusuf said. "We'll have to go down the cliff again soon, onto the Conca d'Oro."

Federigo nodded. Immediately, he knew what Lothair would do: He'd ride along the cliff until he found the most likely place for them to descend onto the plain around Palermo, and there he'd wait. Obviously they couldn't go down the cliff at the most likely place. He fidgeted. He wanted to get back, and it was going to take time. Looking up at the sky, he willed it to rain, and hard.

B E CAREFUL, it's slippery."

"I can't see anything."

"Just follow me, it's not hard." Federigo's bare foot skidded on the rock, he nearly fell, and he caught himself just before he would have gone off the cliff. The rain pounded down on his head and shoulders and sluiced over the stone his feet and hands rested on. It was so dark he could see nothing more than an arm's length away, and the wind kept trying to pluck him off the cliff. He wondered how close they were to the bottom. The cliff wasn't high, and it wasn't steep, but it seemed that they'd been climbing down for hours. He clenched his teeth and slid around a lump of rock that beetled out over the road. Maria, as usual, was praying and crying; and Yusuf was carrying the baby.

"It's ending," Yusuf said softly. "Little Red—"

"I know." The rain was letting up, and he could see more. He tried to move faster. The knights were probably ahead of them, and he needed the rain to hide them when they sneaked past. He slipped and sat down hard, and pebbles and dirt rattled off down the slope. Getting up, he groped with his feet for a way down.

It was getting lighter—he looked up at the sky and saw, past the windy rain, the clouds running pale gray. This was bad. He sidled along a ledge and, to his own surprise, stepped out onto level ground.

"We're down."

"The rain's stopping." Yusuf came up beside him and handed the baby back to Maria. "How are we going to get past the knights?"

"Come on." Federigo ran across the road to the ditch on the far side. It was running water, muddy and deep, dragging branches along with it. Federigo let himself carefully down into it. The water swirled up to his waist; it was cold, and he gasped.

"It's deep, watch out."

"We'll catch cold and die," Maria wailed. She stood on the bank, looking down. Yusuf slipped into the ditch and held up his hands.

"Give me the baby and come on."

"I won't." She stamped her feet. "I won't; I can walk back now."

"No," Federigo said. "The knights know you; they'll take you prisoner. They'll question you. Come with us. It's not bad." His teeth were chattering, and he tightened his jaws.

"Oh—oh—" Maria gave the baby to Yusuf and started into the water. Suddenly she lost her balance and fell with a splash between them. Yusuf held the baby up out of the water, laughing, and Federigo pulled Maria to her feet.

"It's cold," she screamed. "Let me out."

"No, you don't." Federigo shoved her. "Start walking." He looked up at the sky; the rain was settling into a steady drizzle. No one would be riding on a day like this, he hoped. He kept one hand on Maria's shoulder to make sure she didn't try to climb out of the ditch, and they waded on toward Palermo.

Federigo's legs and feet started to get numb. He waded as fast as he could to keep warm. The level of water in the ditch was falling, fortunately, but the ditch was getting deeper; where before their heads had been even with the top, now the road was far above them. A dead branch slithered past him, and Maria screeched.

"It's a branch."

"A snake—it's a snake—he bit me—"

Federigo pulled the branch out of her skirts and threw it up toward the top of the ditch. "Keep going, or I'll beat you up."

Maria stared at him, open-mouthed. When he raised his fist and made a horrible face at her, she whirled and scrambled on, pushing Yusuf ahead of her. Federigo grinned, wondering why it had taken him so long to think of that. The water was down to his knees now, and while he walked he rubbed his thighs to get them warm again.

Tiny streams joined the water in the ditch, and they crawled under a little stone bridge, holding hands to keep the suddenly fierce current from towing them off. The baby wailed constantly. A little beyond the bridge, they passed a tavern. From the roar of noise it was packed full of travelers caught in the rain. Federigo dragged Maria and Yusuf out of the ditch and let them sit on the mud while he sneaked up to the back of the tavern.

It was a long, low building, half of stone, half of wood. The back stank of horse manure, and he could hear horses stamping and kicking in the lean-to just the other side of the manure heap, which was steaming under the light rain. Ducking between two wagons, he found a window and peeked in. All he could see was a fireplace with half a dozen pots hanging over it, and servants rushing back and forth. But he could hear men laughing and shouting, and someone, off to one side, was playing a lute and singing. He thought of the warmth and food inside and started to shiver. Creeping around the corner, he stuck his nose over the sill of another window.

There, at the far end of the room, drinking morosely, stood four knights. They were all sopping wet—one stood in a puddle, his cloak dripping steadily into it. Lothair wasn't with them. Federigo saw a plate of roast pig and his mouth watered.

He thought he knew where Lothair was—waiting at the foot of the cliff a little way from the tavern, in a place where a landslide had made the descent far, far easier than the place they'd actually come down to the road. Lothair would have no reason to wait anywhere else; he wouldn't know that Federigo knew the knights would be waiting for him. Federigo turned and went back through the yard of the tavern, circled the manure heap, and trotted over the beaten grass to Yusuf and Maria.

"Just a little way, now," he said, and slid back into the ditch. Maria started to protest and stopped, shrugged, and followed him. Now she carried the baby, which, to Federigo's relief, was asleep. He waded on through ankle-deep

water toward the city; in the west, the clouds had broken
up, and through a patch of sky the flat red rays of the set-
ting sun poured like a blessing.

"There's my house," Maria said. She clutched the baby.
"It's all dark."

"They're asleep."

"They're dead. The bandits killed them." She walked
slowly across the street toward the gate in the little fence
around the house, and Federigo and Yusuf withdrew into
the doorway of the building behind them. Yusuf whispered, "Shall I go home now?"

"Wait a minute. We ought to go tell Durante's father
what happened to him."

"I will. They live just down the street from me. If you
wander around, someone will recognize you. You should
go home."

"I—look."

Maria had gone through the gate and walked slowly up
to the house and knocked on the door. Now it opened, and
a spill of golden light poured over the girl and the baby, and
someone just inside the door shouted with pleasure. Maria
rushed forward into the arms of a young man. Other people
crowded around her, laughing and embracing her. The
baby, naturally, let out a howl. The door swung shut,
blocking off the light and the happiness, but now light
showed in the windows of the house.

"She's such a silly goose," Yusuf said.

"Well, she was far from home, and she thought they
were all dead, all her family, and we did make her do a lot
of odd things." Federigo scuffed his feet against the stone

threshold of the doorway. "Are you going home?"

"Yes. I'm going to get beaten to a pulp for running off, too."

"No," Federigo said. "They'll be too glad to have you back."

Yusuf said, "Do you want to come home with me and go to the palace tomorrow?" He was already edging away down the street, all the eagerness in him straining him toward home.

"I'll go back now."

"I'll see you tomorrow, and we'll go tell Durante's father." Yusuf whirled and ran off. The slap of his feet faded into the dark.

Federigo sighed. Everybody was glad to have Maria back. Everybody would be glad to have Yusuf back. But he had to go up to the palace, where every corner was full of whispers and conspiracies, and nobody really cared about him except Franciscus; to the rest of them, he was just a thing, a bundle of flesh and bone and blood with a tag on it that said "King." He thought of Hadji-Mustafa and the bandits on the beach, the wanderers in the gully, Lothair on the road—he'd rather be anywhere but home. His head down, walking slowly, he drifted down the street and around the corner.

Palermo was all quiet, all dark. He crossed the square of the Roman Fountain and scooped up a palmful of water to drink. A dog barked at him from the garden of a house he passed, and pigeons cooed from under the eaves and in the bell tower of the Cathedral when he walked by. The wind whispered in the palm trees.

The palace gate was closed. He climbed over it and

dropped down into the park. One of the deer saw him and stopped, its flag-shaped ears twitching back and forth. He walked up to the courtyard and let himself in through one of the little gates in the low wall.

The courtyard was empty, too. Inside the stables, a horse kicked its stall with a crack like thunder; up in the keep above his head, a light moved at a window. It all looked so lonely, so lost. The King was dead, that was why. Or so they thought. He wondered if Diepold were still Regent. He had to be, if Lothair was scouring the roads; Lothair would fall when Diepold fell. He went to the huge main door and pushed it a little way open.

The oak door, bound in iron, swung noiselessly on its hinges, and he squeezed through into the great hall. Up at the far end, lit by torches that were never allowed to go out, stood the enormous throne with its stone canopy carved with the images of hawks and lions. Above it, painted on carved wood, hung the arms of Hohenstaufen, the Norman Kings of Sicily, and the Empire. That was his throne, and those were his arms. Suddenly he felt very small, very dirty, and hungrier than he'd ever been in his life. He went to a side door into another room and opened it.

This room was full of people. Diepold was there, talking to a priest; and Tommaso of Celano, the Count of Molise, who never came to court events—even he was there, surrounded by retainers, gorgeous in silk and jewels that spat light over his clothes. Secretaries scribbled at their desks, and court officers stood leaning against the wall. They all looked exhausted. Federigo walked over to Diepold.

"Have you been looking for me?"

Diepold turned, looked down, and stared. His mouth fell open, and his normally red face turned dead white. Federigo glanced around; all the others were watching him, their eyes bulging out of their heads. Nobody made a sound.

"Where—" Diepold began, hoarsely, and stopped. He looked over toward the Count of Molise. His voice rang with relief. "You wanted the King? Here is the King. Do you see him?" His hand fell to Federigo's shoulder.

"I'm hungry," Federigo said.

"Where have you been?"

The Count of Molise came over and bowed. "Your Grace. Everyone has been much worried about you. Where have you been?"

Federigo said, "I'm hungry. I'm not saying anything until I get something to eat."

Diepold grabbed him by the shoulders. "Where were you? Do you know what you've caused? Do you know—"

Furious, Federigo shouted, "I'm hungry! Feed me!"

Diepold jerked, amazed. The Count called, "The King is hungry. Bring meat and wine and bread for him." Looking down at Federigo, smiling, he said, "You're very dirty as well, your Grace."

"If I want to be dirty, I'll be dirty, my lord." Federigo swung around. "Someone bring me a chair."

All of them rushed up with chairs. Diepold shook his head. "A tantrum." He sat down on his heels, and Federigo climbed into a tall chair; a page held out a plate of peach tarts. Diepold said, "If it please your Grace, where have you been?"

Federigo stuffed tarts into his mouth. Around them, he

said, "I went to Cefalu." A cup of wine appeared, and he
gulped it; and instantly his head started to spin.

"It might not be wise to allow the King to get drunk,"
the Count said. "How did you get to Cefalu, your Grace?"

"On a ship. And I walked back." Federigo remembered
to eat slowly. "I went because I heard that someone was
going to try to kill me."

Diepold frowned; his head turned toward the Count.
"Did you indeed. And who, when he was found to be gone,
was so quick to say he'd been murdered?"

The Count smiled, and smiled, and said nothing. Federigo
looked up at him, startled. He'd thought the murderers
were of Walter of Brienne's party, but now . . . he took
a piece of lamb from a platter and ate it. Diepold stood up,
facing the Count.

"You were so sure he was dead, my lord. You were so
sure we would have to find another King. And who better
fit than the greatest lord in Sicily?"

"Are you accusing me of anything, German? He says he
heard. How did he hear? He's lying, he's making up stories."

Federigo said, "I overheard men talking in the pleasure
house. I don't know who it was. Diepold, leave him alone.
There is no proof."

The Count looked down at him. "Thank you, your
Grace, for championing me."

Inside his chest, Federigo's heart felt encased in ice. It was
the Count, he was sure of it. There was nothing to do about
it, of course. He ate and drank a little more wine, watching
the Count smile at Diepold. The mob of men around him
were all murmuring behind their hands; and their slippery
eyes searched over him and Diepold and the Count, greedy

for something they might use in their own advancement. Which to support, which to betray. Federigo pushed aside a plate of cookies; he was angry.

"I wasn't lying," he said, and slid off the chair. "I'm going to bed now. In the morning I'll tell you whatever else you want to know."

Diepold said, "I'll escort you, your Grace." He glared around the room. "You are all dismissed. What we were talking of is of no importance now, anyway." He started toward the far door, and Federigo followed him.

In silence, they walked through empty rooms, darkened for the night, to the stairway. Halfway up the stairs, Diepold said, "Why didn't you come to me? Why did you run off?"

"I didn't know if you could protect me," Federigo said. The thought of his own bed, of a mattress and covers, made him weary to the bone. They climbed another flight of steps.

"I knew you weren't dead," Diepold said. "I had every man in my army out looking for you."

"I saw them." Federigo looked up the winding stairs. "How did you know I wasn't dead?"

"I know you," Diepold said. "I remember what happened that time I kidnapped you from Markwald of Anweiler, how you screamed and fought. If anyone had tried to kill you, you would have raised an uproar fit to waken the dead." He looked down at Federigo, grinning. "And I heard nothing but silence, the night you ran away."

Federigo laughed. Suddenly there were feet running on the stair, and with a swirl of robes Franciscus sailed down the steps toward them.

"Federigo! I heard you had come back—"

Federigo threw his arms around Franciscus and hugged him. The familiar smell of ink and soap filled his nostrils. "Franciscus, Franciscus, I had an adventure. Did you miss me?"

"I was so frightened for you—" Franciscus hugged him so hard his ribs cracked. "Federigo, you almost broke my heart."

"I'm sorry."

"Sweet Heaven, you're filthy. You need a bath, have you eaten? You must be exhausted." Franciscus set him down, looking him over, and suddenly hugged him again. Federigo began to cry with pleasure.

Diepold was going back down the stairs. "Make him look like a king again, Franciscus, I need him tomorrow to sign charters." On the landing, he paused and looked up. "I missed you too, Federigo." He made a face, as if admitting it hurt him, and went off down the stairs.

Franciscus hustled Federigo up toward their chambers. "How did you get so dirty? Where did you go?"

"I went sailing, and I met—oh, so many strange people. And a witch." Federigo went into his room, peeling off his clothes, which were stiff with dirt and sweat.

"Did you learn anything?" Franciscus shut the door.

"Yes." Federigo looked around. Everything was the same, so familiar and so welcome that he laughed. "I learned how to splice lines on a ship, and how to . . ." It occurred to him that he'd learned something else. He sat down on his bed. "I learned a lot of things."

"Anything important?"

"Yes. I think so, but I'm not sure what it is. That I can do what I want, but first I have to do a lot of other things." He frowned. "I'm not sure what I mean."

"That you have to earn your freedom?" Franciscus held his shirt out at arms' length. "Well, go to bed. In the morning, you really have to have a bath. And we have many lessons to catch up with."